A Man Called Friday

Helene Hadsell

Updated by
Carolyn Wilman

Copyright © 2008 by Helene Hadsell, Delta Sciences LLC
Copyright © 2023 by Helene Hadsell, revised and updated by Carolyn Wilman,
7290268 Canada Inc., dba Idea Majesty
All rights reserved.

Although the author and publisher have made every effort to ensure that the information in this book was correct at press time, the author and publisher do not assume and hereby disclaim any liability to any party for any loss, damage, or disruption caused by errors or omissions, whether such errors or omissions result from negligence, accident, or any other cause.

All rights reserved. No part of this publication may be reproduced, distributed, or transmitted in any form or by any means, including photocopying, recording, or other electronic or mechanical methods, without the prior written permission of the publisher, except in the case of brief quotations embodied in critical reviews and certain other non-commercial uses permitted by copyright law. For permission requests, contact the publisher:

7290268 Canada Inc., dba Idea Majesty
info@ideamajesty.com

For details on quantity orders, contact the publisher at orders@ideamajesty.com.

Paperback ISBN: 978-1-7773194-1-0
eBook ISBN: 978-1-7773194-2-7

Cover design by Mark Lobo of doze!gfx.

DEDICATION

To Helene as she shared her life's adventures with all of us.

Helene Hadsell
June 1, 1924—October 30, 2010

ACKNOWLEDGMENTS

Helene Hadsell
I appreciate the time and talents of both my dear friend, Shirley McKee, and my granddaughter, Melissa Bittner.

MORE BOOKS

To read articles and stories from Helene Hadsell's archives, along with other adventures, audio programs, and videos, all for FREE, visit www.WordsForWinning.com

BOOKS BY HELENE HADSELL

The Name It & Claim It Game

In Contact With Other Realms

Confessions of an 83-Year-Old Sage

A Man called Friday

https://bit.ly/HeleneHadsellBooks

BOOKS BY CAROLYN WILMAN

You Can't Win If You Don't Enter

How To Win Cash, Cars, Trips & More!

https://bit.ly/LearnToWinSweepstakes

ONLINE WORKSHOPS

WINeuvers for WISHcraft 2.0

Sweepstakes for Beginners

How to Win Giveaways on Social Media

RoboForm 101

http://bit.ly/CQWorkshops

TABLE OF CONTENTS

Dedication	iii
Acknowledgments	iii
More Books	iv
Carolyn's Foreword	7
Helene's Introduction	9
Sazz Speller	11
The Skylarks	19
Buck Garcia	45
Olivia Roundtree	61
Trish	85
Thomas Braden	89
Adam	101
A New Beginning	131
Epilogue	143
About the Authors	145

A Man Called Friday

Carolyn's Foreword

I am not sure when I first heard about Helene Hadsell, but sometime in the early 2000s, I was gifted a used copy of her first book, *The Name It & Claim It Game*. I felt fortunate as it had not been in print since 1988. I devoured it.

It wasn't my first introduction to positive thinking, visualization, mental projection, goal setting, etc. When I turned eighteen, my dad gave me my first motivational book, telling me, "If I can teach you at eighteen what I learned at thirty-six, you'll be way ahead of me."

After years of self-study, I concluded that my purpose was to teach others two things. First, how to bring more fun and excitement into their everyday lives by winning sweepstakes, and second, how to utilize a wide range of metaphysical methodologies and teachers—like Helene—to achieve that magical life.

I started my teaching path in 2004 by writing a book: *You Can't Win If You Don't Enter*, and also by publishing a newsletter. Then in 2008, I added a blog and a podcast to my platform. Every other Monday for several years, I chatted with the movers and shakers in the promotional industry, eager to share my message.

As I was always seeking dynamic guests for my podcast, I reached out to Helene, and she agreed to be on my show. I was beyond excited. (The audio interviews were recorded and can be found on my Contest Queen YouTube channel, along with an entire video playlist here: https://bit.ly/HeleneHadsellPlaylist.)

After our first interview, I was pretty brazen and bluntly asked Helene if I could come to Texas to meet her in person. She said no. A few days later, I received a phone call from her inviting me to visit. She said my spirit guides were so loud that she had to concede. (I am loud in life, so it didn't surprise me that my spirit guides were also loud.)

That November, I found myself in Alvarado, Texas, in the presence of this remarkable woman. To me, women like Helene were the original teachers of spirituality. Helene had mastered not only the

Law of Attraction but also the art of manifesting, along with many other extraordinary metaphysical skills. It's that very mastery that she imparts in all of her books. Helene also felt 'if she could do it, you could do it.'

During my visit, she suggested that I pick up her gauntlet and start teaching others what she had been teaching for decades. She didn't see herself teaching in person again and didn't want her messages to pass with her. I didn't do anything with her suggestion until now.

Because I interviewed her, wrote about her, and shared her teachings over the years, I received many requests for her books, courses, and Blueprint readings. Finally, it was time for me to stop holding the gauntlet she'd given me and start running with it.

I contacted Helene's family and received permission to update and republish her books. I was beyond excited to be putting out into the world what this intelligent, vibrant, and gregarious woman asked me to do over a decade ago.

It is important to me that I maintain the integrity of Helene's work, so I've only made minor adjustments in this edition. I've reformatted her books for current publishing methods (Print On Demand, Kindle, Kobo, Google Books, and Apple Books).

I've also made it easy for you to distinguish Helene's words from mine. **All of Helene's are in the Arial font.** All of mine are in the Times Roman font.

Helene called this type of novel a FACTION as it was a combination of fact and fiction. If you read any of her other works, I am sure you will spot the instances where Helene weaves in her metaphysical interests and life experiences, blended with her fantastical imagination, as well as catching glimpses of her eclectic personality peeking through some of the characters.

It's my hope you enjoy this story as much as Helene had writing it.

Carolyn Wilman
Marketer, Author, Teacher

HELENE'S INTRODUCTION

NOTE: I discovered this note by Helene in the remains of her files. I do not know when she wrote it, but I wanted to share it because it gives you a glimpse into how she came to write her only work of fiction. This was the last book Helene published before she passed away in 2010.

I had just finished writing the book; **Confessions of an 83-Year-Old SAGE** when I asked myself, *"What's next?"*

My mind goes in so many directions I have to stop and slow down to focus on one thought at a time instead of being bombarded with six or seven ideas. A Man Called Friday will be the title of my next book. This will be fiction. In the past, I have written only non-fiction.

I stayed busy creating scenarios for the character. The idea came to me after going through my library as I searched for a book that might spark my interest. Robinson Crusoe, which has been a classic for every young reader, caught my attention. The book was written by an Englishman and published in the eighteenth century. The story tells about how a native on the island where Robinson Crusoe landed after his ship was wrecked became his manservant.

My story would be about people who had the opportunity to have the use of a man called Friday for an entire month to do their bidding. After completing three episodes, that would be considered a short story; I finished it. *"Now, what next?"*

A Man Called Friday

SAZZ SPELLER

The receptionist announced, " Alex Sander to see you, Mr. Speller."

As he was ushered through the big mahogany door, Alex Sander wondered what he was getting into if he agreed to accept the position offered by author Sazz Speller. The ad in the Houston Chronicle read:

> Wanted: Male, forty to fifty years of age. Must be free to travel with no family obligations for a one-year contract. Sense of adventure, ability to do field research required. Call Beth for an interview at: 888-555-6363.

His curiosity aroused, Alex made the call and memorized the details given to him.

"A sense of adventure" kept running through his mind.

Sazz Speller, the author of six bestsellers, was searching for the right person to do research for his next book, to be titled *A Man Called Friday*.

In his late sixties, frail but dignified, Speller sat quietly behind his cluttered desk. Most noticeably, he had little hair except for a patch of gray around his ears. His eyes were closed.

Alex stood silently, waiting for something to happen, feeling that Speller must have put him on hold.

Abruptly, the old man cleared his throat. "I'm not asleep, just resting my eyes." A slight smile spread across his wrinkled face as he opened his eyes, those extraordinary blue eyes that one could gaze into and see forever. Then, for a moment, Speller studied Alex as strange and disquieting thoughts raced through his mind.

There was something about this man, this Alex Sander, that was familiar.

"Have a seat, Mr. Sander, and I'll explain what kind of person I'm looking for to help me with my next book. If you like the idea and we can reach a meeting of the minds, you may be my man called Friday."

Opening a notebook, he turned several pages until he found what he was looking for.

"Ah, here it is," he said, nodding his head. "Hear me out, and then you can ask questions."

Speller began, "This started when I shared the seed of the idea with my friend, Baxter, who owns eleven radio stations across the country. I wanted to sponsor a contest, and Baxter agreed to help me; he's always looking for good public relations ideas for his stations. The prize will be the services of a man called Friday. Friday will live with the winner of the contest for an entire month. His job is to be available and assist the winner in ways that will make an ordinary person's responsibilities easier—sort of like a full-time servant." Speller's eyes sparkled with the possibilities and scenarios that could unfold.

"The contract we'll give the winners will stipulate that we have the right to use the notes 'Friday' takes of the experiences as they happen for the book I'll write. I think there could be a lot of unique and exciting material."

"There are a lot of reasons people might need a man called Friday. They might need a jack-of-all-trades, a babysitter, a companion, or maybe even someone to do windows. Possibly a gun for hire?" He laughed as he watched Alex's expression. "Seriously, what I'm looking for are unusual requests. How does the idea strike you?"

Before Alex could answer, Speller continued, "Oh, yes, anyone can enter the contest. The rules are to submit a hundred-word, or less, essay stating why they would like to have the services of Friday. I will judge and have the final say who the winners will be. Any questions?"

Speller's gaze riveted on Alex's face, then moved over him slowly, sharp and assessing, searching for Alex's reaction and still puzzling over why he looked so familiar.

"Why yes, I have several," Alex replied. "How did you come up with the idea? It sounds interesting. Something I'd like to do. 'Friday,' Yes, I could handle that."

Speller picked up a copy of Robinson Crusoe and handed it to Alex.

"Ever read it?" Speller asked.

"It's been a long time." Alex nodded as he paged through the book.

"It was written by an Englishman and published in the eighteenth century. It became so popular I venture to say the entire English-speaking population has read it or at least heard of it. I've always liked the idea of giving someone the opportunity to have a person at his or her beck and call. I'm talking about a middle-class person, not the affluent. The idea has been percolating in the back of my brain ever since I began writing. Also, I have a dear friend who refers to his loyal secretary as his girl Friday. I'm curious to find out what people from different walks of life need to make their daily routines more comfortable. Does that answer your question?"

"Yes. It answers one of them. Your ad mentioned the position required traveling."

"The radio stations that are promoting the contest are located all over the United States, so the winners may live in different locales. Is that a problem?"

"No, I was just curious. Do you anticipate that there will be any foreign travel?"

"No, I lived overseas so much that I probably understand the Asian peasant better than I do the American middle or working class, so the research will be in the United States. At any rate, the station personnel are enthusiastic about cooperating. They will do the preliminary judging—reading the entries and weeding out similar requests before they send their selections to me."

Speller then fell silent for so long Alex wondered if his mind had wandered off on some long road into his imagination. Finally, Speller lifted his head and asked, "Why did you answer my ad?"

"Curiosity. I'm looking for a new frontier, if you will. I'm forty-four, recently divorced after twelve years of marriage. I took a leave of absence from my accounting firm just to step off the treadmill I've been on since I got my MBA twenty years ago. I've been with the firm for fifteen years, a partner for ten."

For a moment, Alex's mind flashed back to his office. The confinement, *the same old, same old*, as the cliché went. He hated the photos on the wall and the smell of everything—the stale coffee in the hall, the chemicals near the copier, the perfume of the secretaries—everything! Alex was a man of remarkably few vices. He did not smoke, overeat, or take drugs. He did enjoy a cocktail now and then. He liked women but was not promiscuous. He believed in commitment in a relationship.

Changing the subject, Alex masked his inner turmoil with a forced smile and continued his explanation.

"I used to be an avid reader, but for the past several years, I've relied on movies to tell a good story. So, I'm not familiar with your books, although I have seen a movie adaptation of your book, Chin's Hidden Secret. It won an academy award, and rightly so.

"I did a little research on the Internet about you. It indicated that you lead a legitimate, if rather offbeat, life, rather like the adventurers you write about. I'm impressed, perhaps a little envious. Now, I'm ready to do some living instead of just existing, to loosen up and go where no man has gone before."

Alex allowed himself a quick chuckle.

Speller was half listening to what Alex was saying. Seriousness lurked in the shadow of his eyes. He felt a kinship with Alex the moment he laid eyes on him, and he had to know why.

"Have we ever met before?" he asked abruptly. "You look so familiar."

"Not to my knowledge," Alex replied, slightly taken aback. "I've never had a publisher or author as a client, and I seldom mixed socially with the literary people in Houston."

"Perhaps it's just someone you remind me of—happens quite often." Speller sighed as recurring questions ricocheted through his mind. He tried to quell them so he could carry on with his meeting.

"Interesting. I don't feel that I know you, but I had a distinct feeling of déjà vu as I came through the office doors. The interior reminds me of my grandfather's office—all the books, the personal photographs hanging on the walls, and the huge, cluttered desk. When I was, oh, eight to twelve, I spent my summer vacations with my grandparents. It always was a fun experience. My mother's job required out-of-state travel, and my stepfather was a police lieutenant in the crime investigation unit, so he worked long and irregular long hours."

Alex enjoyed recalling the pleasant memories. "Grandmother was on the Library Board and was in charge of the weekly Story Time program. Her passion was to encourage everyone to read. Now that I think about it, that's when I read Robinson Crusoe. She provided a gathering place for kids my age. Because she didn't drive, on some afternoons, we would walk uptown, and that always meant a stop at the drugstore soda fountain for ice cream. And then, another stop by my grandfather's office on the square."

Alex smiled as he remembered that his grandmother always spoke of his grandfather as "The Judge." She was proud of her status as his wife in their small community.

Speller was relaxed and seemed genuinely interested, so Alex spoke slowly, letting the memories flow. "Both are gone now, but the memories of the good times I had with them are still with me, always will be, I suspect." He sighed, then added, "They were very special."

After a moment's pause, he continued, "Speaking of memories, here is something I'm curious about—your statue of Quan Yin. I noticed it on your patio. My mother has a miniature bronze of the standing goddess. It has always been displayed in a prominent place in our home. Several months ago, when I visited Mom, I saw that it was still on the mantle. We discussed it briefly, and I once again asked her why it was so special. She explained that Quan Yin is a mythical icon in Asian culture, pouring out compassion on the world. For me, it's a reminder to practice compassion. Mom gave me her secret smile, patted me on the shoulder—as was her custom as far back as I can remember—and added, 'One day you'll understand.' She isn't a Buddhist but a lapsed Presbyterian, and I still have no explanation."

A flicker of startled recognition flashed across Speller's face. He wanted to know more but decided to give it some serious thought before he jumped to conclusions and made an ass of himself.

Hastily, he replied, "I discovered my Quan Yin in a Chinese market when I relocated to Houston. I've had so many special and fond experiences with the people I spent time with in Asia I had to have it for my office. So—to answer your question—it's a reminder of those times."

Speller took a deep breath and said abruptly, as seemed to be his custom, "Young man, I've made my decision. The job is yours if you want it. I can start the ball rolling today. If you accept my offer, I feel that you will make a significant contribution to my story."

"Yes, I accept." They shook hands across the desk on the agreement.

Alex's eyes were lit with an inner fire. He was excited at the prospect of a new and possibly very interesting direction in his life.

"My profession requires research and report writing," he told Speller. "It will be interesting to use my skills in a new field."

Speller nodded.

Alex's heart danced with eagerness. "When does this all start?" he asked.

"It's already in progress. In fact, I received five letters in the morning mail." Speller opened a file and pulled out a letter.

"I told the station managers that I wanted to see the original letters. I can tell a lot about a person from his or her handwriting."

"This letter has the entire staff at the radio station in Tennessee interested. It's from a man that lives in Wind Ridge."

Speller handed the letter to Alex.

"Someone put 'NOTE! Ray Skylark will make a good story' at the top of the page. Sounds like they know the man. From the tone of his letter, he may not have too much education, but sometimes, book learning isn't that important if one has common sense. Read it and tell me what you think."

Alex leaned back and slowly scanned the letter.

Hello,
My name is Ray. I have two sisters, Faye and May. We are up in years—slowing us down some. I'm writing about that Friday fella, to help me get some things done around here.
I heard he is free on your radio.
We will feed and water him good. Treat him kindly.
The girls don't know I wrote this. I want it to be a surprise.
I'm the champion card player round hear. If you do us rite, I'll tell my secret how I always win.

Ray Skylark
Wind Ridge, Tennessee

After Alex read and reread the letter, he turned back to Speller and asked, "What else do you know about this man?"

"Guess the staff at the radio station told Baxter about the letter because he was on the phone with me this morning. He said the guy had become a recluse and had been out of circulation for the past two years. He knew that the Skylark family inherited the Slone place when the family drowned in a storm at sea. The Skylarks and their children were the Slone's servants for over 50 years."

"Why would he want a stranger to come and stay with him for a month?" Alex asked, searching his own mind for a plausible explanation.

"Maybe he needs someone to help him do repairs around the place. Baxter said that he must be in his early seventies and that his two sisters are around the same age." Speller, too, was obviously weighing the question. "This request has Baxter all fired up. He told me that the station has a pickup and a travel camper that you are welcome to use. It's one of those self-contained models that just requires hooking up to electricity."

"That was thoughtful. Sounds like Baxter really would like to know more about the Skylarks."

Alex pursed his lips. He found it curious as to why Baxter showed more than a passing interest in this particular letter.

As though he had read Alex's thoughts, Speller said, "I'll admit my curiosity is aroused, too. Knowing Baxter as I do, he must sense a really good story for publicity. I'll bet that's it."

Speller was silent for a moment, then added, "If you decide to take this assignment, I'll have Beth, my administrative assistant, contact Skylark directly and get more details."

Alex smiled. "The offer to teach me how he always wins at cards has my curiosity aroused. It just might be interesting."

A week later, Alex got the call from Beth. She had all the information necessary on the Skylark file. The only thing she needed from him was the date he wanted to leave.

"Mr. Speller would like to meet with you tomorrow. Will two in the afternoon be convenient?" she asked.

"That will be fine. I'll be there."

Alex had spent the interim catching up with friends and making a quick trip to visit his mother, who lived in Cincinnati. She was pleased he had found an interesting new job. She had been concerned about him after his divorce. He had seemed so restless and unhappy.

She wanted to hear more about Speller after reading his books that Alex had given her.

"He sounds interesting," she said.

THE SKYLARKS
RAY—FAYE—MAY

Speller enthusiastically greeted Alex when he arrived at his office. "Beth has gathered additional information for your first assignment." He picked up the report as he motioned to a chair and began reading parts of it aloud.

"The town's population is one thousand, eight hundred and sixty-two. It's an old town established in the 1890s. Never did grow too much due to the mountainous region."

The writer-side of Speller came out as he embellished the report. "It sounds like a place where county building codes, weed ordinances, or waste-disposal regulations don't carry a lot of weight. People live as they please. There are still a lot of small towns that fit that description."

Alex sat and absorbed the information as Speller continued describing the place.

"Wind Ridge is exactly sixty miles from Nashville. There is a city park where they still have band concerts performed by the local high school band. There's a library, two family restaurants, a grocery and drug store, and, of course, a McDonald's." He glanced at Alex and nodded. "The place also has a tourist draw. The Skylarks have a gift shop that features tobacco leaf crafts and molasses made by local residents." Looking up from the report for a moment, he repeated, "Tobacco leaf crafts? That sounds different."

"I'll check it out," Alex murmured. "It does sound original.

"This comes as quite a surprise," Speller said, a tone of awe edging his voice. "We will be getting a lot of help from Baxter's staff. Since Baxter, for whatever reason, has taken a personal interest in this assignment, and he himself will be on vacation in Europe with his wife, one of his staff will meet your plane with the pickup truck and travel camper for your use when you land in Nashville. He will have specific directions on how to get to Wind Ridge, including a detailed map that will take you directly to the Skylark place. Sounds like he has covered all bases," Speller said, looking up from the report to hear Alex's comment.

"I like having the use of the truck if I want to explore the place. How far is the Skylark place from town?"

"Let's see—seems I read it someplace. Yes! Here it is! Twelve miles from Wind Ridge. There is a larger town in that vicinity called Newport. It's sixteen miles from Wind Ridge. That place probably has a hospital, theatre, motel, and more nightlife, if you need a getaway."

"Tennessee is one state I know little about, not being an Elvis fan. I've had no reason to go there." Alex gave a sheepish grin when Speller looked at him.

"You'll need a laptop for your reports and a cellphone to contact me if there's an emergency. We'd better check to find out if reception is good in that area. I understand it's in a valley surrounded by mountains."

Speller paused, then started to laugh. "Good heavens, I sound like a father sending his son out on his first scout camping trip."

They continued to discuss the details, and it was at that point that Alex's practical side surfaced. "I do have another question. We've not discussed the details of daily living—my salary as Friday. And, incidentally, from now on, I'm calling myself Friday. Might as well get used to using the new name." He grinned.

Speller smiled. "I guess wages would be an important part of this, wouldn't it?" He chuckled and added, "...Friday. Okay. The winner will receive a check for one thousand dollars at the end of the month to defray any expenses incurred during Friday's visit. Your compensation will be paid separately from my office. This first assignment will be an experiment—no need to set a lot of rules until I know how it plays."

Speller animatedly explained, "That's what is going to make this story I plan to write so engaging. I'm a people watcher. Each person has a unique personality. What makes a person click, tick, get sick? Are they mad, sad, bad, or glad? Are they serious, silly, or sermonish? What I enjoy most about people is when they have an offbeat sense of humor. That will be up to Friday to discover and relay to me."

"I do require that you keep a daily log about the winner, his associates, and his environment. At the end of your stay, you will send me a summary of your impressions, and we can meet to discuss it if I need any additional information." He raised his eyebrows and gazed at Friday, "Any more questions?"

Friday shook his head, and for a few moments, they sat in mutual anticipatory silence.

It was decided that Friday would leave the following Monday.

In her customary efficient manner, Beth would complete the arrangements and contact the radio staff as to when to meet his plane.

Jordan, the man who met Friday at the airport, had no problem recognizing him. From the detailed description, Speller had given him.

The plane was two hours late due to mechanical problems, and Ray Skylark was expecting Friday before dark.

After Friday picked up his luggage, they headed for the parking lot. Clouds were gathering. Jordan handed Friday the keys and said, "I'd give anything to be in your shoes. I'm curious as to why Baxter finds the Skylarks so interesting."

"Speller and I were wondering about it, too. I'll have a whole month to learn the answer." Before driving away, he added, "I'll fill you in on the details when I return the truck."

It began to rain as Friday left the parking lot. The rain hit the windows in taps and splatters, small and countable, and then suddenly, it was everywhere, banging loudly on the roof of the truck.

The highway was only a mile from the airport, and once he got on it and headed toward Wind Ridge, he sat back, relaxed, and listened to the different sounds—the engine of the car, the traffic as it rolled

A MAN CALLED FRIDAY

by, the swish-hum of the tires on the wet pavement and the metronomic thump of the windshield wipers.

He was happy and content, looking forward to meeting the Skylarks.

Little did he realize what was in store for him.

By six o'clock, he exited the highway. The rain had stopped as he turned onto Route 4W. By half past the hour, he was in Wind Ridge, and twelve miles later, he drew up under a sign that read SLONE ROAD.

Turning down the country road, it looked abandoned by all but postmen, lovers, and Boy Scouts. The limbs of trees hung low over an oiled dirt surface, and from the bushes came the keening of locusts.

Even though the rainstorm had now passed, drops still fell from the low-hanging trees onto the truck.

According to the map, the Slone property was bound on three sides by this road.

He stopped to study the map again and noticed it indicated a road into the property nine-tenths of a mile farther along. It was like a treasure hunt, he thought.

Driving slowly for overgrown hedges and trees that leaned into the road, he finally saw a gap in the laurel and there, in just the right space, stood a pair of pillars almost totally obscured by ivy. Time and weather had bleached most of the printing on the mailbox that stood on one side, but the last five letters remained, although dim. They were unquestionably "y-l-a-r-k."

Aiming the truck between the pillars, his first day with the Skylarks began.

A small jungle of undergrowth and a graveled driveway lay on the other side, and then the laurel thinned and a huge expanse of lawn, grown wild with yellow mustard, lay before him.

At the crest of the lawn, some distance to the right stood a house bristled with turrets, gingerbread, eaves, gables, and porches.

"WOW," Friday gasped aloud. "The size, the view, the trees—this isn't a house; it's an estate."

Friday drew up beside the front porch. As the engine died, he noticed the old man sitting in a rocking chair on the porch. It had to be Ray. His hair was such a pure white that, in contrast to his weather-beaten skin, it appeared to glow like a nimbus around his head.

With his equally radiant goatee, his kindly features, and his compelling black eyes, he seemed to have stepped out of a movie about a jazz musician who, having died, was on earth once more as someone's angelic guardian.

Friday had not expected to see a man with such dignity. Based on the letter he had read, he pictured Ray Skylark as a hillbilly in bib overalls, straw hat, and corncob pipe—a Grand Ole Opry character.

Boy, was he mistaken. Ray was wearing a smart short-sleeved button-up with matching trousers and loafers.

After getting out of the truck, he walked toward the porch steps and, looking up at Ray, he smiled and said, "I'm Friday—at your service."

Ray stood up, extending his hand. "You don't know how glad we are to have you here," he said as he shook Friday's hand.

The front screen door opened, and a wrinkled little old lady beamed at him with a smile that lit her entire being.

"You must be the man the radio station sent. Ray tried to keep your coming a secret, but secrets around here are a lost cause," she said jokingly.

"I'm Faye, the oldest of the three Skylarks," she explained. "Come sit on the swing with me." She walked lightly to the end of the porch, where a newly painted green swing hung from the ceiling beams. She felt the seat. "Good, it's dry. Ray painted it last night to brighten up the place."

She laughed as she adjusted a pillow on the bench. "I need a little padding nowadays to keep this body comfortable."

Ray sat back in his rocker, smiling as he let his older sister take over the conversation.

"Might as well be upfront with you," Faye said. "I'm seventy-two, our sister May is seventy, and Ray is sixty-eight. So how old are you? You look like a strapping strong young fella."

Ray's eyes glowed with pleasure as he watched Faye enjoying herself. Friday was also enjoying Faye's friendly chatter. He immediately liked these two people.

"I'm forty-four." He reached into his front shirt pocket and pulled out a notepad.

"Ray, do you mind if I take notes? It will help me in my report to Speller."

"Of course not," Ray answered casually.

Friday jotted down their ages in pencil and then motioned toward the yard. "I see that you could use a yardman, and I like working outdoors. By the looks of it, this place will give me that opportunity." He turned a page and began a list of chores he saw needing to be done. Neither Ray nor Faye was shy about giving Friday chores to add to his list.

Friday could feel Ray studying him while he wrote, much the way Speller had, not that it bothered Friday much. He just wished he knew what they were thinking.

When he was done, he looked around, expecting to see the other sister appear. "Where…"

"May is the cantankerous one," Ray informed him as if reading his mind. "She is having one of her childish days. You just have to learn to ignore her when she gets into one of her moods."

"Ray," Faye said, her tone turned serious. "We really should prepare him for May. We don't want him to have any surprises."

Ray nodded. "You see, May is getting to be somewhat of a challenge. For your safety, I suggest that you stay on guard. She is unpredictable and can be a danger to herself and anyone around her."

"What do you mean?" Friday asked, his eyebrows furrowing with concern.

"She has mental problems and should be institutionalized, but we can't bring ourselves to do that," Ray said sadly. "She still has a lot of good days."

Friday nodded, not knowing how to respond exactly. He changed the subject by asking where he should park his travel camper and if he could hook up to their electricity.

"Show him around the place, Ray, and I'll finish supper." Faye got up to go inside.

Ray led Friday through the flower garden. The camper was to be parked beside a gazebo, sorely in need of repair. "Looks like I need to cut back some of this wisteria," Friday said as he tried to plug the extension cord into the outlet. He made a mental note to add that to his list.

"The tool shed has all the equipment we need to tame this forest," Ray said. "I've been mowing and hedging, but since May is getting to be more of a handful, I've let everything go."

Inside the shed, every imaginable type of tool hung neatly on the walls. An ancient-looking riding lawnmower rested just inside the door. Friday hoped it was in running condition.

He reached up and lifted a hedge trimmer from its wall hook. "This will do the job for now. I'll get to the rest of the yard work in the morning."

Handing Friday a key, Ray said, "We keep the shed locked at all times."

After Friday hooked up the electrical plug, he and Ray headed toward the front of the house. But when Faye called, telling them that supper was ready, Ray showed him to the back door. "This way," he indicated to Friday.

"What a handy idea," Friday said, indicating a small sink on a maple chest beside the back door. A row of finger towels hung on a rod attached to the wall.

"This was one of Mrs. Slone's ideas," Faye told him. "She was a neat freak. Servants had to wash their hands constantly. It does come in handy to wash your hands before eating. By the way, did you notice our big vegetable garden?"

Friday admitted he hadn't.

"I hope you're a vegetable lover," Faye said, laughing, "because that's pretty much all we eat in the summertime."

The kitchen was spacious and had a large round maple table sitting beside a window that looked out over a flower garden.

"It's more convenient to eat in the kitchen these days," Faye said as she set bowls of food on the table.

Friday was hungry when he sat down to eat. It had been six hours since his last meal, and Faye had prepared everything he liked—a huge green salad, fresh tomatoes, squash, biscuits, and an egg-spinach casserole.

He hadn't known what to expect. In fact, when he passed McDonald's in Wind Ridge, he decided if the meals were not up to his liking, he could get fast food or try out one of the two cafes in town.

No doubt about it, Faye knew how to cook—definitely a plus. He smiled as he began his feast.

"Save room for a peach cobbler," Faye said, getting up to bring it to the table.

As Friday spooned a serving into his bowl, he heard the tormented cry of a cat. Out of the corner of his eye, Friday saw Ray stiffen. Suddenly, a small woman broke the ominous spell by pouncing out of the hallway into the kitchen naked, on all fours.

Her long fingernails clicked on the tile.

She scampered into the corner and crouched there, gazing evenly at Friday.

Her eyes were like the eyes of some reptilian hunter that had been around since the Mesozoic Era and knew all the tricks.

Then, with a sudden self-consciousness that was almost comical, she feigned nonchalance, curled up into a ball on the floor, yawned, and turned her eyes to Faye as if to say, "Who me? Lose my feline dignity? Don't be ridiculous." She turned her attention to the back of her hand and began licking it slowly and deliberately.

Surprise siphoned the blood from Friday's face as he sat and witnessed this petite woman's mad behavior. He turned to Ray, struggling to keep his face from betraying the fear that had surfaced.

Ray got up and walked over to the creature on the floor. He patted her on the head and, in a soothing voice, lulled her into a relaxed mood.

"You're hungry, aren't you, May? Faye will get you some milk."

Faye left the table and poured milk into a small bowl, and sat it in front of her sister. She, too, patted May's head.

May lapped the milk with her tongue, all the time keeping her reptile eyes on Friday. When she finished, she crawled out of the room.

The three sat in silence for a moment. Then Faye abruptly began explaining. "It's something she just started doing recently. She thinks she's a cat. We've been trying to figure out what prompted that behavior; then we remembered that, as a child, she had a cat and would mimic it. We thought it was just child's play."

Faye bent her head, obviously distressed for her sister.

"One never knows what's going on in her head," Ray said. "It seems harmless, so we humor her." He closed his eyes as though trying to shut out the scene that had just occurred.

After an uncomfortable pause, Friday thanked Faye for the wonderful meal and, glancing at his watch, said, "It's after nine, and it's been a long day. I think I'll go to my camper and get some sleep. I want to get an early start on the yard tomorrow."

He stood and left the room, thinking, *what have I got myself into?* He walked out into the warm night.

Darkness enveloped the yard, except for a meager patch of murky yellow light from a poorly maintained and grime-dimmed security lamp.

Friday felt he was being watched, and he quickened his pace toward the camper. Once inside, he bolted the door and heaved a sigh, relieved to get away from the scene he had just witnessed.

He pulled out his laptop to log the experiences of his first day as Friday. Writing it down did nothing to relax him, as the memory of May's shocking behavior kept him on edge and tense.

He spent a restless night as spasms of fear wakened him. Time and again, he was certain he heard scratching and meowing at the camper door.

"Get hold of yourself," he kept repeating.

The morning sounds of birds awoke him. It was shortly after 6:00 a.m. when he drew back the curtains beside the bedroom wall. Might as well get up and get started, he decided, and he began exploring to see if there was anything in the cabinets.

Coffee…coffee…he hadn't thought about it until he was ready for his morning cup. Sure enough, someone had thought about it. Inside one cabinet was a can of Folgers and a gallon jug of spring water. He sat and drank his coffee, quietly ruminating over the dinner scene the night before. He half contemplated calling Speller and leaving this assignment, but he couldn't bring himself to do it. He's been intrigued by the promise of adventure, and that's exactly what he was getting.

Once he had finished his coffee, he left the camper and headed for the tool shed. He could begin clipping the hedges around the walk before anyone got up.

He was wrong. Ray and Faye were on the back patio, nursing their coffees as he turned the corner.

"Breakfast will be ready in five minutes," Faye chirped, as cheerfully as the birds flitting and feeding at the nearby feeders.

"Let's eat on the patio," Ray suggested. "I'll help you with the tray, Faye."

As they ate, Faye seemed in such a cheerful mood. She talked nonstop about the people she called her friends who lived in town. "It's been about a year since I attended a social, but I have my good time memories to reflect on," she said, sipping her coffee.

When it seemed she was finished reminiscing, Friday asked, "Don't you have anyone who comes to help?"

Faye answered, looking to Ray for support. "We did, but when May became too aggressive and unpredictable, no one wanted to come. It's pretty much been Ray and me that have been keeping this place up, as well as taking care of May."

"And there were several instances that happened in town that people gossip about," Ray added. "I might as well be honest with you, Friday. We no longer have any friends. They are afraid to come around, and I don't blame them. I can live with it, but Faye misses being with people. That's why I wrote that letter to get you to come and visit us."

Friday sat and listened intently. Ray studied him for a moment before he continued. "Next week, I want Faye to go to Newport for several days to visit friends. I can handle May, but I just want someone here in case I need help. If May gets to be too much, I can lock her in her room."

"I'll do whatever it takes to help you while I'm here," Friday assured him. His concern quickly turned to sympathy.

Changing the subject, Friday rose and announced, "I'm ready to get this yard looking like a showplace. I can visualize how it must have looked in the past. Does the riding mower work?"

"She runs like a top." Ray's mood shifted from serious to light-hearted as he followed Friday to the shed.

Friday spent the day doing yard work while Ray and Faye tended the garden. It was a productive day for Friday. He got a lot accomplished. Ray and Faye expressed pleasure with all that he'd been able to do that day.

After supper, they sat on the porch watching the fireflies prick winking holes in the fabric of the night.

"I've always been fascinated by fireflies," Faye said, reflecting on her obviously happy childhood. "As a kid, we caught them and put them in a glass jar, took them to bed with us, and watched them until we fell asleep."

Friday wanted to learn more about the Skylarks. It was now obvious that they were well educated, so why did Ray write a letter that belied his true self? Friday wouldn't be comfortable with this until he knew the answer, and the only way he could think of to approach the subject was to just come right out and ask.

"Ray, your letter interested my boss, Sazz Speller. When he read it with all the misspelled words, his comment was, 'He may not be well educated, but he used common sense when he wrote it.' So would you mind telling me what prompted you to deliberately sound 'hillbilly'? I guess that's the word that comes immediately to mind."

Ray threw back his head and let out a great peal of laughter. "So he is wise to me and still granted my request? Well, I'm glad he did. It means a lot to me." Quickly changing the subject, he asked, "Tell us a little about yourself."

Friday answered Ray and Faye's questions and told them about the newspaper ad, his feeling that he needed a change in his life, Speller's novels, and how he came to take the assignments as 'Friday.'

The Skylarks were genuinely interested.

"Now," Friday said, "it's your turn to fill me in about the Skylarks."

"I'll let Faye tell you our family secrets," Ray replied.

Faye laughed. She had a light melodious laugh that was pleasant to hear.

"You asked for it. My life's ambition was to meet a handsome prince, get married, and raise a big family. It never happened."

She paused, shook her head a little sadly, then added, "Guess it does for some people, but my destiny moved into another direction. But let me start from the beginning."

She straightened herself with dignity. "We were fortunate that our parents were servants for the Slone dynasty. The Slone family and their forefathers raised tobacco. We grew up on this property. There were two houses—we lived in the one located two hundred yards behind this place. We called this one 'the big house.'

"Our home burned down eight years ago, struck by lightning. Because the Slones had no children, the three of us—Ray, May, and I were treated like their family. Ray and I went to college, and May met and married a career navy man during her first year in college."

"Mrs. Slone taught Ray to play the piano and later had him take private lessons. May and I had a voice tutor. This all began when I was ten and Ray and May were younger. We evidently fulfilled her expectations with our talents because we became the attraction and entertained at their parties. Ray played and wrote some excellent songs, and May and I were a duet. I sang soprano. May has a lovely alto voice."

"After Ray and I finished college, Ray went to New York to continue his profession in music. He played at some of the popular supper clubs. He knows a lot of famous people. I used to visit him occasionally."

"I chose to teach music at the high school in Nashville. After our father died and my mother was in ill health, I moved back here and taught at the local high school."

"May was traveling around the world with her husband. When they divorced, she moved back home and opened a gift shop in town. She is very creative and made some of the most interesting dolls, flowers, and pictures using tobacco leaves. You must go see the place when you go to town. We sold the shop a year ago."

Faye seemed to enjoy telling the details of her family background, and Friday was totally intrigued.

"There is more," she said, "but let's take a break while Ray opens a bottle of wine and I get the scones I made this afternoon."

After Ray poured the wine and they all settled back with the delicious scones, Faye continued her story.

"The Slones had many wealthy friends, and they went on a number of business trips. They were one of the major growers of tobacco at that time. Every summer, they took a fishing trip with one of Mr. Slone's partners. A storm at sea capsized their boat, and all of the passengers and crew were lost at sea. We were shocked when we were told that we had inherited this property."

"Ray moved back here to oversee the place. I guess he missed giving performances because he talked May and me into singing as we did as kids. I had no idea that we would get bookings to entertain. People actually paid to hear us."

She laughed a looked at Ray. "At first, we did clubs in Nashville, and then we had a contract to entertain on cruise ships. It was an exciting time; well, at least it was for me. I must show you our *Ego Wall* in the den where all our pictures with famous people are displayed."

After a brief pause, she shut her eyes momentarily and continued, "We began noticing that May was having mood swings; her personality would change so abruptly that she seemed like a different person. Several of our sponsors accused her of using drugs. I was close to her, and I knew that was not the problem. She finally agreed to go for an evaluation—a brain scan and all the tests that are now available these days. Tests showed lesions on her brain, which is not a common occurrence. There's no magic cure—medicine or treatment. The prognosis is bleak. She still has good days when she is her true self. I'm sorry you had to see her at her worst last evening."

Friday absorbed her words without question, consumed with an insight into the information he knew little about.

"Today, she is in her room rocking and singing to a doll. We think she slips back into the time when she did have a child. Her little girl died at the age of two." Faye sighed as if a burden had been lifted off her shoulders by telling the story.

"I just want to have one more 'hurrah' for May before the time comes when we have to make our final decision to have her committed," Ray added sadly, gazing out into the dark.

Abruptly, Faye stood up, clapped her hands, and said, "Pity party time is over. I'm in the mood for music." Turning to Ray, she said, "Let's do our *hot-to-trot* song for Friday."

"This calls for a glass of brandy. We sound better with a drink," Ray said, grinning. "The wine will keep."

Ray took up the change of lighter conversation with a sigh of relief and led Friday inside and into the den, where a piano and sofas filled the spacious room.

"Friday, are you ready for a performance by the Skylarks?" Faye joked.

As Ray began to stroke the piano keys, she looked at Friday and asked, "Do you like Hoagy Carmichael, Jerry Lee Lewis, or Liberace? We aim to please."

"How about all three?" Friday said. "I'm familiar with their music, and I like them all, so surprise me."

He enjoyed the way Faye could shift gears, and he was ready for this change of pace.

Ray ran a few scales on the keys. "I need to warm up. It's been some time since I played." As he began a song and Faye joined in with the vocal, Friday sat back, relaxed, and listened, impressed by their talent.

Suddenly Ray looked up; his eyes widened with astonishment as May entered the room. She walked over beside Faye and began harmonizing with her just as they had done so many times in the past.

Friday sat spellbound. When they finished the song, May turned to Ray and said, "Let's do *At The Same Time.* It's a song Barbra Streisand and Celine Dion sang together."

When the Skylarks had finished the song in their perfect harmony, it would have been a draw as to which duet gave a better performance. They were sensational.

Friday stood and applauded, yelling, "Brava! Brava!"

May looked at Faye and asked, "Aren't you going to introduce me to our guest?"

"This is Friday. He'll be staying with us for a month. He came all the way from Texas to help Ray with the yard work" Faye brightened with pleasure as she nodded her head, looking to Ray for his response.

"A professional gardener! What talent do you have? Perhaps changing weeds into flowers?" May's laughter was contagious as she took over the conversation, asking questions and making plans to go to Jimmy's Crab Shack for lunch tomorrow.

"We are going to Nashville tomorrow, aren't we?" she pleaded with Ray.

"I don't see why not," Faye chimed in. "We can even stop by the German bakery and get several loaves of their black bread we all love."

"Then it's settled. We will leave about eleven to be there for lunch," May announced. She turned and left the room. Ray and Faye stood for a moment and watched her leave.

His voice breaking with emotion, Ray said, "Friday, I want you to remember May the way she is tonight."

When Friday left for his camper that night, he had a lot to think about. He had never experienced such a drastic change in a person. How long would she be normal? And what about tomorrow's outing? As sleep began to overtake him, he found himself wondering if tonight might signal a repeat pleasurable episode for their planned trip.

The next morning, after breakfast, Ray suggested that they wash the Lincoln. Friday anxiously waited to see May or have an update on what mood she was in. He wondered why she hadn't joined them for breakfast.

Faye answered his questions without being asked. "May is in good spirits today. She's trying to decide what to wear."

"Is it okay if I wear jeans?" Friday asked, hoping it wouldn't be too informal.

"Sure," Ray replied. "That's what I'm wearing."

After they finished washing the car, Friday left to change his clothes.

"I'll honk when the girls are ready," Ray said.

Faye and May were seated in the back seat when Friday opened the front door to get in. The leather creaked behind Friday as he pushed back the seat to get comfortable.

He turned his head to greet May.

When she saw him, she screamed, "Is that thief still around? He came into my room last night and stole my broach; the one Daddy gave me on my fifteenth birthday. You remember?" She looked at Faye, then reached over and grabbed Friday around the neck, yelling and screaming, "You dirty thief! Give it back to me!"

Fear overcame Friday. Ray reached over, trying to loosen her grip as Faye helped pull May back into the seat.

Faye handled the situation by telling her that the broach was on the table in the house. "Let's go get it," she suggested.

May was finally placated enough, and both women got out of the car and went inside. Ray followed.

They had succeeded in calming May down, but Friday was another story. His heart was still pounding, and he felt as if his rib cage had become a vice that was squeezing his vital organs between its jaws.

He opened the door, got out, and placed his palms on the top of the hood, gulping in deep breaths, trying to compose himself. He had never felt so much fear. It was a totally new experience for him. Expect the unexpected came to mind as he stood waiting for Ray to return.

In a few minutes, Ray did return. "Are you all right?" he asked. "She didn't hurt you, did she?" Embarrassment was evident on his drawn face.

Still shaken, Friday answered, "It was so unexpected. I got caught off guard. I'm okay. Are you sure Faye can handle her?"

Ray replied, "I'm certain. It's happened before. She would accuse her customers of stealing when she owned the gift shop in town. It got to be so embarrassing we finally sold the place. Let's put that behind us and make this a man's day off. Faye insisted we go as planned." Ray settled into the car and waited for Friday to do the same.

As they headed for Nashville, the conversation turned to family, women, marriage, and children.

"Have you ever been married, Ray?" Friday asked.

"I'd have liked to have had a family and at least three or four children," Ray answered, "but it wasn't in the cards. I'm an accidental celibate. It was granted when I was twelve years old. I woke up one morning with tenderness under my right jaw. It got worse, and I developed a fever. It was mumps, the doctor said. A week later, the swelling, to put it delicately, had moved below my equator. Even lying in bed was painful. After a time, it was established that I was sterile and to be denied the joy of children."

After that intimate confession, Friday felt compelled to tell Ray about his compulsive disorder, making lists and note-taking. When Friday finished his confession, they both enjoyed a good laugh.

As the saying goes, they bonded.

After lunch at the Crab Shack, Ray took Friday on a tour of the city.

They passed the Ryman Auditorium, the former home of the Grand Ole Opry. It was closed, but a gift shop nearby had enough Opry memorabilia to fill a museum.

"No, not interested," Friday said when Ray asked if he wanted to stop and look around.

They did stop at a bar where Ray used to play piano. The bartender recognized Ray and was genuinely glad to see him. Drinks were on the house, and Ray extended his drinking past the limit for safe driving.

"You be the designated driver," Ray suggested, handing Friday the car keys.

And Friday took the opportunity to ask something he had been waiting for Ray to suggest.

"I'm not a card player," Friday began, "just played some Bridge when I was married, but I'm curious about the comment you made about always winning at cards. Is there a secret? Or were you just joking?"

"I'll admit to winning ninety-nine percent of the time. It's a combination of reading people and doing your homework before you play with the big boys. Did you ever see the movie *The Hustler?* It was a Newman movie. It described to a 'T' my buddy that I roomed with while I lived in Greenwich Village. That was in my younger days. His friends and I called him The Hustler because that is what he was. He was able to read people."

"Reading people takes practice. Their every eye movement, hand gesture, smile, or nod are clues. Sitting next to the player is also helpful. You are in their energy vibration. Some people call it their aura. You can pick up if they are excited, disappointed, or neutral. I notice if they perspire, clear their throats, or breathe shallowly. We used to refer to a player as an N-H—Nothing Hidden, a C-H-L—Cool Hand Luke or a G-H—Green Horn. There was a group of four of us that sparred together every free minute we had. We shared our insights with each other. Anytime one of us met a guy that wanted to do some serious playing and said he felt lucky, it was just a matter of time before one of us was able to peg him. I never was a professional player. Two of my friends are still on the circuit playing in casinos all over the world. But that's another story."

"Everything has a formula, and the formula for being a winner is to know all you can about your opponent. It's not luck—it's practice. While you're here, if you seriously would like to learn more about yourself and people in general, I'll be glad to share with you all that I know. That is if you treat me R-I-T-E." Ray pronounced each letter as he spelled it out, then looked over at Friday as a flash of humor crossed his face.

"Yes, I'm interested," Friday replied. "When do we start?"

"Why not this evening? Faye enjoys playing, and she is no G-H."

It was going to be more interesting than Friday had first expected. They rode in silence for a moment. Suddenly, Ray cleared his throat and, expressing his serious nature and said, "Over the past several days, I've come to know you, and I want to be straight with you. The real reason why I wanted and needed a total stranger here is for Faye's benefit. She has finally admitted that May is too much for both of us to handle. This has been going on for the past two years. It's only become more difficult these past three months. As I told you earlier, I persuaded Faye to take a two-day break and go to Nashville. What she is not aware of is, shortly after she leaves, two male nurses will be coming from the private sanitarium that I have already contacted to take May away. In order for her to cooperate, they will sedate her to make her leaving safer and less traumatic.

"I'm sure that Faye is aware, on some level, of my plans. It's just that if it were up to her, she could never release her. That's where you come in; because you are a guest, you will be able to support me, to make it easier for her to adjust after May is gone. I know my sister better than she knows herself."

Friday listened quietly, at a loss for words.

As they entered the driveway, Faye came out to meet them, walking with purpose.

"Uh-oh, something must have happened while we were gone," Ray said as he stopped the car and quickly got out.

Faye looked stricken, and her words tumbled out. "May has locked herself in Friday's camper, and she won't come out. I tried bribing her, but it hasn't worked. I'm just concerned that she may think she is a cat and destroy the inside." Turning to Friday, visibly shaken, she said, "I'm so sorry, Friday."

Ray interjected, "I'm concerned if there are any knives or anything she could hurt herself with."

Ray went on to explain that May had attacked him several weeks ago with a knife. "She thought I was a burglar. It wasn't serious, but I'm more alert now."

Friday recalled seeing two sharp knives in one of the drawers in the camper.

"There are a couple of knives in the kitchen drawer," he ventured, becoming more apprehensive just thinking about it.

"She is getting more aggressive. We have our knives and sharp instruments locked up. Ray keeps the tool shed locked for that reason," Faye said, her face clouded with anxiety.

"Do you have a key?" Ray asked, the tensing of his jaw betraying his frustration.

"Yes, but it's inside the camper on a hook by the door. I should have thought of that and locked it. I take responsibility for not being more careful," Friday said awkwardly, clearing his throat.

"No!" Ray insisted, "If anything is ruined, we will replace it. It is our responsibility."

What had started out as a look-forward day was fast becoming a nightmare, unraveling around Friday. Ray and Friday went to the camper to examine the door, trying to figure out how to open it.

It was made of metal and impossible to open from the outside. They checked the window, but Friday had closed the curtains that morning before he left, and they were unable to see inside.

"She has to come out sometime. Let's let her be for the time being," Ray suggested. They all traipsed back to the house.

Faye fixed sandwiches, but no one ate very much.

As it grew dark, Faye and Ray went over to the camper door, trying to coax May to come out and listening for any sign of movement.

Nothing.

Friday stood by, feeling helpless.

It was after 1:00 a.m. when Ray suggested that Friday sleep in the guest bedroom upstairs.

He had no other choice. Faye brought him a fan in case he got too warm.

Ray again cautioned Friday to be on guard before saying goodnight.

39

There was no lock on the bedroom door. Friday pulled out his notepad and frantically began to jot down the things that were spinning around in his mind, so he might keep them straight. He started to play the "What If" game.

What if she got out of the camper with a knife and came after him?

What if he was off guard and had no way to defend himself?

What if she destroyed the computer he left inside the camper?

What if she trashed the camper?

A helpless feeling overtook him. Suddenly he remembered when he was in college and did not want to be disturbed; he would prop a chair under the doorknob. He did so now. It worked. Now, could he sleep?

☐☐☐☐☐

Outside, the sky was brightening from black to gray-black. Dawn hadn't crawled out of its hole yet, but it was creeping close, and it would crest the mountain horizon in ten to fifteen minutes.

Friday couldn't stay in bed a minute longer. He'd spent a restless night curled into a tight knot of muscle and bone, hugging himself to ease the strain across his tense shoulders. Then, forcing himself to relax, muscle by muscle, joint by joint, he tried hard not to imagine what May was capable of doing.

He got out of bed and went downstairs. Faye was making coffee, and Ray was taking a shower.

"I'll go and keep an eye out to see if she leaves the camper," Friday volunteered as he walked toward the door.

"She never did turn on the lights," Faye said as Friday left.

Friday was just approaching the camper when he saw her. She was lying face-up on the gazebo steps.

He stopped.

She might be playing possum.

But then he noticed the blood and the knife still lodged in her stomach. As he cautiously drew closer, he could see that her eyes were open. He stood a moment, turned, and walked toward the house to get Ray.

Ray was just coming out of the door when he saw Friday and immediately knew something was terribly wrong. He walked toward the camper and saw her. He stood there for a long time in silence.

Both Friday and Ray occupied themselves with thoughts of what they should do or say next. It was Ray who broke the silence. "I'll call the sheriff. There'll be an investigation, and we'll have to wait for an autopsy. It's standard procedure." He took a deep breath and let it out in ragged gasps.

"I'll have to tell Faye," he said. "I have no idea how she'll handle it."

They needn't have worried. When Faye heard the news, she remained calm, much to both Friday's and Ray's surprise.

She stood for a moment as if trying to decide if she heard right. Then she turned to the two men. She picked the telephone off the cradle and handed it to Ray.

"Do you want to call the sheriff, or shall I?" she asked.

A sense of strength overcame her and lessened the despair; her newly awakened sense of life comforted her. Powerful relief filled her.

Ray watched and understood.

◻ ◻ ◻ ◻ ◻

After the preliminary investigation and all the reports were written, the sheriff, who was aware of May's mental condition, turned to Faye and said, "You did more than was expected. She finally found peace."

When the ambulance drove away, Ray and Friday went over to the camper. Both were relieved that there was no damage.

That evening as they sat on the porch, Faye, searching for a plausible explanation, said, "I think she knew what she was doing the moment she slipped away to go into the camper. She was searching for a way to end her life. The knife was her means to an end."

41

There was a memorial service at the local church. Ray played the organ, and Faye sang the hymn *Dwelling With the Angels.* There wasn't a dry eye in the congregation. The townspeople were kind, calling and stopping by with food and flowers. Throughout the entire event, Faye was very quiet.

Friday was concerned that she was masking her suffering with this contrived calmness.

"She'll be all right," Ray assured him.

A week later, Faye announced that she was ready to liven up the place. She put Friday and Ray to work painting and cleaning all the windows. She went through every room, dusting and rearranging things.

She made a list, longer than any that Friday had ever written, for things that needed to be done.

Ray and Friday pitched in, and the place was transformed from dull to dazzling.

Their evenings were spent on the porch, and both Faye and Ray shared their insights with Friday about reading people.

They played a number of games of blackjack. On Friday's last night with the Skylarks, they played poker, and Friday finally won. He figured it wasn't his skill that Ray had let him win. Ray denied it, but by then, Friday could tell that Ray was a C-H-L and that he wasn't going to pursue the issue.

He learned so much in such a short time he was grateful for having had the opportunity to meet and spend a month with them—as strange as the month was.

Friday drove directly to the radio station in Nashville to deliver the truck and camper after he left the Skylarks.

The radio station's personnel were eager to hear all about his experiences. They were shocked to hear the news about May while he was there.

Friday learned that Baxter had personally interviewed Ray Skylark on two previous occasions about his music.

"Did you find out how he was so lucky at playing cards?" Jordan asked.

Friday smiled and replied, "N-H, Nothing Hidden, C-H-L, Cool Hand Luke, or a G-H, Green Horn player."

Jordan laughed and began, "Skylark very briefly discussed his card playing in one of his interviews. When Baxter kept trying to pursue the subject, Skylark cleverly switched topics back to his music. This really disturbed Baxter."

"I can imagine," Friday said.

"Baxter said, 'This guy is a card shark, but couldn't get him to admit it. I'll bet Skylark wrote his entry letter in that hillbilly tone as a joe on Baxter—to see if he remembered who he was," he mused.

Jordan continued, "Baxter never lets things rest. When we showed him the letter Ray wrote to get Friday's service, Baxter made it a personal project to find out more about him. Baxter is presently on a European tour, but he left instructions to keep him informed."

Jordan shook his head and grinned. "Why do I keep feeling that Baxter and Skylark played cards together and Skylark beat the pants off Baxter? You didn't hear that from me."

"I hope that puts closure on it for Baxter if that's what happened," Friday told him. *Speller will be glad to know he used body language to win at cards*, he thought.

It was time for Friday to leave for the airport to catch his flight back to Texas. He would let Speller again thank Baxter for the use of the camper.

As Friday relaxed and lay back in the airplane seat on his journey back home to Texas, his thoughts turned to the card playing.

I wonder if Speller plays cards.

A Man Called Friday

Buck Garcia

Friday found himself more comfortable this time in Speller's office. It was almost like he had known the author all of his life. And his exciting experience with the Skylarks had only whetted his appetite for more experiences as A Man Called Friday. He really enjoyed getting to know people, whereas before, he had been consumed by his numbers-oriented job at the accounting firm. He enthusiastically shared his experiences with Speller.

Speller pulled a letter from the growing stack in his folder.

"This one really got my attention," he said. "It comes from Buck Garcia, an overseer of migrant workers in South Texas. He writes that he is always short-handed for the orange-picking season. His postscript is what really got my attention. I quote, 'Your man called Friday can eat all the fresh produce and oranges he wants.' The letter was printed with a pencil on lined notebook paper. It was both the paper and P.S. that made this letter different. Think of the possibilities living among migrant workers. So many personalities to observe. Yep, he will be the next winner." Speller added.

Friday smiled. "He does sound interesting. My Spanish is pretty rusty, and I don't know too much about the food production industry, but I'm willing to learn."

It was vegetable harvesting time at Hallway's Truck Farm when Friday stepped off the county rural bus.

Buck Garcia was there to meet him, wearing an old pair of scuffed loafers and a white starched shirt, unbuttoned at the neck.

A dark shadow of stubble covered his cheeks, chin, and neck. His black hair was ragged at the edge. His shoulders were as broad as any linebacker's, but they sagged as if he carried the world's problems.

He was, to Friday, a huge man, at least six feet four and well over two hundred and fifty pounds.

"Howdy, Friday," he greeted him in a gruff but friendly voice.

45

Friday was immediately aware of Buck's South Texas drawl. Buck cleared his throat, then started a long series of hacking coughs. The outline of a pack of cigarettes was plain to see in his breast pocket.

"You're a sight for sore eyes," he shouted after the coughing fit subsided. Buck grabbed Friday's hand and began shaking it. He almost lifted Friday's six-foot, one-hundred-ninety-pound body off the ground.

"I'm putting you up in the cabin next to the bunkhouse where the workers stay," Buck said. "I'll see that you're well taken care of."

He grabbed Friday's duffel bag as Friday bent down to pick it up. Buck tossed the thirty-plus pound bag into the bed of his pickup like it was a sack of feathers.

The drive was less than twenty-minutes. As they drove, Buck talked a steady stream about the crops, glancing sideways to study Friday's reaction to the information he was giving.

Friday sat quietly, listening as he felt himself surveyed and evaluated under Buck's gaze and trying hard not to feel uncomfortable.

It was equally awkward for Buck. It was the first time he'd been boss to a gringo. What, he wondered, was he getting himself into?

When the two arrived at the Hallway's farm, they went directly to the cabin that would be Friday's home for the next month.

It was clean and livable with a single bed, a chest of drawers, a sixty-watt bulb hanging from the ceiling, a square table with two chairs in the middle of the room, and a ceiling fan above the bed.

Buck stood for a moment, lost in thought. Suddenly he crossed the room and pulled back a flowered curtain.

"The bathroom," he announced.

The four-by-eight room was an obvious afterthought, probably added when the luxury of indoor plumbing arrived at the ranch. It housed a rusting metal shower stall, a sink, and a toilet.

"This place is used when one of the hands has a visitor. Two days is the maximum that anyone can stay here," Buck explained in an authoritative voice. "You're an exception. This is your place for the next month. Take your time to settle in while I take the crew's time sheets to the boss man. Tomorrow is payday." He raised his chin with authority as he strode toward the door. "I'll be back in a couple of hours to pick you up in time for chow."

The screen door slammed behind him.

Friday stood in the middle of the room, looking around for a closet where he could hang up his clothes.

The casual suit he wore on the trip was his main concern. He gave a low sigh of relief when he noticed the three hooks with wire coat hangers by the door. After hanging up his suit, he opened his bag and put the contents in the chest of drawers—a camera, a hand-held tape recorder, two notebooks, and six notepads. As an afterthought, he had stopped by the bookstore to get two of Speller's novels. He needed to familiarize himself with his employer's writing style.

Buck returned shortly before noon. Friday had changed into work clothes, and he noted that Buck had changed his clothes, too. He had opted for an armless sweatshirt and blue jean shorts. A red plaid bandanna hung from his hip pocket.

"You're in for a treat," Buck said with a wide grin. "Rosie and her daughter, Avelia, cook for the workers. I asked her to make enchiladas today. Their cooking beats anything I've ever eaten in any fancy restaurant. Rosie is an even better cook than my woman is, but you didn't hear that from me."

Friday stifled a smile as he reminded himself, "Don't let this guy's size fool you. He's a pussycat." Beneath his soft side was a man with immense character and physical strength.

☐☐☐☐☐

The mess hall was built beside the bunkhouse where the single men stayed.

Married men and women workers had to find a place of their own in town. They arrived at sunup each morning, packed standing in the back of a rattletrap cattle truck.

The setup reminded Friday of the time he spent in Guatemala for a month as a volunteer for the Peace Corps.

Workers on the farm were served two meals a day, breakfast at sunrise and lunch at noon. The mess hall remained open the rest of the afternoon for anyone to come in and help himself to trays of fruit, leftover tortillas, or Mexican hard rolls.

There was also a refrigerator holding a variety of cold cuts and cheese. Cold sodas were kept in a dilapidated Coca-Cola commercial drink machine.

"Alcohol is not allowed on the premises," Buck told Friday. "What they do off the property is their business."

"Ow," Friday said with a grin. "I'll have to substitute a Big Red or Coca-Cola for the Bud," he joked as they filled their plates and sat down to eat lunch.

Friday had rejoined the bar scene since his divorce, seeking the company of other bachelors. A game of darts or talking baseball with his neighbor Brett in the corner pub over a beer or scotch and soda passed the early evening hours and postponed going home to an empty apartment. Before he left Houston, he told Brett about his new venture and promised that he would touch base when he got back home.

Friday snapped back to the present when Buck pushed his plate aside and began telling him that the boss was anxious to meet him.

"Entering the contest was actually my wife's idea," Buck said. "That woman just flat insisted that I oughta write that letter. Truth be known, I never thought I had a chance in hell of winning." A thoughtful smile curved his lips.

Without warning, Buck stood up, picked up a spoon, and clanged it against his glass. When the room quieted, he announced in fluent Spanish, "Listen up, men. For the next month, I'll have the services of a helper. His name is Friday, and he is here to help me keep an eye on you."

The crew laughed. Several nodded to Friday and immediately went back to their plates of food.

That taken care of, Buck turned back to Friday. "You'll meet Mr. Hallway tomorrow. He's coming by for lunch. I told him I didn't put you on the payroll and that you are here to help me out. You can explain to him about the radio contest if you don't mind."

Friday nodded. "Sure. And how long have you been working here?" he asked, pulling a small reporter's notebook out of his pocket.

"Eighteen years. I've worked all three places at the Hallway family farms. When I first started, I never knew which farm I'd be working on, but for the past five years, I've been the overseer on this farm. I started here when I was sixteen and came over from Mexico with my father and two brothers for crop picking. He seemed proud of his accomplishments. "After I married, I bought a little place up the road from here. My father and two of my younger brothers still pick for Mr. Hallway. He is a good man to work for; he helped us get our citizenship papers."

Buck stretched, flexing his elbows. "We've been here all this time. I'll be thirty-four come July." Buck Garcia was proud of his job, and it was obvious.

"Wait a minute!" Buck frowned. "What're you writing down?"

"Just a few facts. It's a long-standing habit of mine. I believe in writing things down. It seems like I can rely more on my notes than my memory. My stepdad was a cop, a detective, and he always carried a notepad with him."

Buck was clearly uncomfortable, so Friday elaborated. "He not only made lists at a crime scene, which he didn't share with me, but he made lists of movies, book titles, telephone numbers, chores, and so on. I was very impressed and proud of him. I began carrying around a notebook as soon as I could write." He paused for a moment. His tone was apologetic. "I'm not sure whether I was just mimicking him or if I have a compulsive disorder. That's what my wife—my ex-wife, that is—called it."

Friday's laugh was weak. He was apologizing too much. "Listen, Buck; if it makes you nervous, I'll close the notebook."

"Nah, it's okay by me, now that I know why you do it. But if you write around the boys, they'll think you are maybe from immigration or the Texas Rangers, and they won't cooperate with you for nothing."

"Glad you warned me, Buck. I don't want to start off on the wrong foot." Friday slid the notepad back into his pocket. He would just wait and make notes later.

After lunch, they got into Buck's pickup and headed for the fields. Friday stayed at Buck's side and helped when he saw the need, refraining from pulling out the notebook.

Maybe it's ridiculous making a list of everything I observe and do, Friday thought. *Maybe I really do have a compulsive disorder. Or, maybe reaching for the pad and pen is just a nervous reaction because I'm out of place here. Or, maybe a nervous reaction and a compulsion are the same things.*

Friday pondered all of this for the rest of the day. He concluded that that's just the way it was and, besides, note-taking was part of his job with Speller. He made a mental note to just be more discreet about it.

It was a long day. After Buck delivered him back to the guest cabin, Friday took a shower and propped himself up on the bed with his computer. Later he would go over to the mess hall and fix a sandwich. Right now, he needed to write down the day's happenings as they had unfolded. He began organizing your thoughts.

Buck's remark about the men being intimidated if they saw him taking notes disturbed him. Now that he had time to give it some serious attention, he recalled that when he went to the pub back home, his neighbor would announce as he walked in the door, "Head's up, y'all. Here comes the detective."

Once he had finished his daily report for Speller, he stretched out on the bed.

He drowsily watched the overhead fan pushing air around in warm, gentle circles; the laziness of it stirred his memory back toward the time his partner embarrassed him at the staff Christmas party, telling amusing stories and incidents that happened around the office when he focused on him.

"I've been privileged to see some of Alex's most private lists and notes, including the ones on which he kept track of every meal eaten and every bowel movement since the age of ten."

He just stood there red-faced with his hands in his pockets and hoped he looked like a good sport. He could feel himself flush just remembering the incident.

The note-taking had to stop. Otherwise, he would look like a fool and make people uncomfortable. After all, he wasn't Colombo.

Decision made, he turned on his side and quickly fell asleep.

☐☐☐☐☐

Friday awoke to what sounded like a foghorn. He guessed it was the wake-up signal. He sat up straight, rubbing his hands together briskly as if he was about ready to chop wood or perform some other invigorating exercise.

Slipping into his jeans and a polo shirt, he headed for the mess hall. Today, he would meet the big boss at lunch. He was looking forward to it. Buck spoke so highly of him; he must be a special person.

The morning went by unusually fast. Friday was shocked when he heard the lunch bell.

Mr. Hallway was already in the mess hall when Friday and Buck walked in. Hallway was one of those people that Friday would have enjoyed doing a thumbnail sketch of; if only he could write it all down. This needed every detail to be accurate.

Hallway looked like a biological clock that seemed to be suffering from chronological confusion. He had the smooth, unlined, wide-open face of a thirty-year-old, the graying hair of a fifty-year-old, and the age-rounded shoulders of a retiree. He wore a white shirt open at the neck and blue jeans. He was already eating when Friday and Buck walked over to his table.

Hallway pushed his chair back and got up to introduce himself and shake Friday's hand. In his haste, he neglected to wipe his hands of the guacamole and sour cream he had been enjoying. Not to embarrass him, Friday quickly wiped his hand on the back of his jeans.

After they filled their plates from the buffet, Friday and Buck joined Hallway, who kept asking questions about the contest. Although he continued eating with gusto, he seemed genuinely interested in how the concept of A Man Called Friday worked.

Hallway reached for a corn tortilla, scooped up a generous glob of guacamole and sour cream, spooned some chopped onions on top, and ate with an appreciation only one step removed from manic glee.

In all of Friday's forty-four years, he had never seen anyone quite like Mr. Hallway. He wondered what the man's parents looked like. He was Anglo, not of Hispanic background. And where did he acquire his table manners?

He sounded intelligent except for the fact that every fifth word was followed by "you know." Friday lost count after he heard it repeated for the twentieth time.

Maybe he wasn't the only one with a compulsive disorder.

Hallway's cell phone rang, bringing Friday's thoughts back to the present. Hallway got up from the table to find some privacy, or perhaps he was finished eating.

Friday smiled. He had run up against a real character, one that would go well in Speller's novels.

☐☐☐☐☐

For the first few days, Buck was reluctant to ask Friday to do anything specific. Friday just followed the big man around and watched what was happening.

He learned there were thirty-four workers and three truck drivers who hauled the loaded crates of vegetables to a nearby processing plant.

This was not one of the bigger truck farms—just a little over 90 acres. The carrots, squash, tomatoes, cucumbers, radishes, and Swiss chard were the vegetables harvested while Friday was there.

The workers moved from field to field as needed. Buck made the decisions when the crops were ready to pick.

Buck stayed constantly on the move, from the packing shed to the field, lending a hand wherever needed. He knew all of his crew by their first names, and the men had obvious respect for him. He had hands-on charge of every job on the place.

On the third day, Buck handed Friday a cell phone and gave him the keys to a truck.

"You can see what needs to be done. Any help will be appreciated."

And Friday pitched in like a pro.

Everything ran smoothly until the day Tony got his hand slashed by a broken wire on top of a crate. To Friday, it appeared his thumb was severed. Buck grabbed the first aid kit but couldn't stop the bleeding. When Tony passed out, Buck and one of the men loaded him on the back of a truck and drove him to an emergency clinic.

Friday served as boss for the remainder of the day.

The following morning, just a little past 2:00 a.m., Friday's cell phone rang. It was Buck. He had been called home. His mother, who lived in Mexico, was dying, and Friday had to take over all responsibilities for the next several days.

"You can do it, Friday," Buck assured him.

And Friday knew he could count on help from any one of the men, who seemed to have accepted him.

☐☐☐☐☐

It was not all work and no play. Saturday at 4:00 p.m., the workers began their weekend off, returning to work Monday morning.

Buck, now back from his mother's funeral, invited Friday to join the festivities and meet his family. Friday asked if it was ok to wear jeans.

"Anything goes," Buck replied.

At forty-four, Friday was still a handsome man. His brown eyes were just as vigilant and passionate as they were when he was on the debate teams during his college years. His voice still carried the same modest warmth and enthusiasm. He had a strong chin and a carefree manner that exuded confidence. His course black hair fell in a permanent windswept tuft across his forehead. When you shook

53

his hand, the callused roughness of his palms might remind one of an accomplished seaman. Actually, they were acquired through his love of the outdoors, chopping firewood and clearing brush around the area of his mountain cabin where one day he would retire.

At Buck's suggestion, the mess hall had been utilized for social gatherings twice a month on Saturday evenings. The tables were pushed back against the wall. The jukebox was on high, vibrating the room with Hispanic songs and music.

Freddy Fender seemed to be the crowd's favorite. Perhaps it was because he was a cousin of one of the workers. Or was it his woesome lyrics?

Besides the jukebox, there was live entertainment, a foursome—two workers, Tony and Richard, who worked for Buck, and two workers from a neighboring Hallway farm formed a band and played lively tunes. They were now warming up in the back.

There was dancing, and the ladies brought food. Even the children were included in the festivities.

A surrounding screened porch was utilized for the children to play games. This didn't deter nor stop them from running back and forth to climb up on their mother's or father's laps. The mothers brought blankets for their young ones to sleep on as they gave out, one by one, after an exhausting day.

When Friday walked into the mess hall that evening, all eyes were on him. The workers' families and friends had heard so much about him from Buck. Buck was enjoying the role reversal, telling a gringo what to do. Friday had almost reached celebrity status.

Buck immediately greeted Friday and led him into the middle of the room, took his arm, and held it high.

Buck turned toward the band, and on cue, they played a drum roll.

Buck announced, "Ladies and gentlemen, my man called Friday.

Everyone stood and applauded.

Buck leaned over to whisper to Friday. "I need a favor. I want you to dance with my wife's sister."

Without giving Friday a chance to respond, Buck stepped away, and a beautiful, slender Hispanic girl wearing a Pueblo dress stepped forward.

The Mariachi band blasted out music with gusto, and she began dancing the flamenco.

Everyone clapped to the rhythm of the beat. Even the children joined in. After she concluded and took a bow, she came over and took Friday's hand, nodded to the band, and pulled him close to her. He had no choice. As the music began, he was amazed at how easy it was to be in sync with her. He felt like he was back in the Peace Corps, dancing with the native people and relaxed into the movements.

When the song ended, bulbs flashed, and onlookers taking pictures surrounded them. Friday found himself uncharacteristically tongue-tied. Sensory overload had set in—the introduction by Buck, dancing the flamenco with a professional, and of all things, finding himself here in the mess hall unexpectedly face-to-face with Speller, Mr. Hallway, and a stranger, who he later learned was Baxter, Speller's best friend from the radio business. He strode over to greet Speller.

"I'm surprised to see you here," Friday said, attempting to recover from an I-don't-believe-it-moment.

"Baxter never lets an opportunity slip by if it means publicity. He called me this morning and insisted we check on our second winner, Buck because he was not able to be there for the first winner. We came in on his chopper."

Speller was obviously enjoying the setup.

"Was Buck in on it?" Friday asked.

"Hell, no! It wouldn't have been a surprise for the two of you. I called Hallway. He suggested that we invite Buck's sister-in-law to dance. She's a professional entertainer, you know," The music had started up again, and Baxter was almost shouting so he could be heard over the din.

While the picture-taking and interviews with Buck were taking place with Baxter in charge, Friday and Speller had time to chat.

"How is it going?" Speller asked. "I know it's only been ten days, and your daily reports are keeping me informed and up to date. It will just be a matter of time before the fellows loosen up more and consider you one of them. That's when their true personalities will surface." Friday agreed, and they talked about Buck's level of trust in him—so much so that he was able to leave him in charge.

While Friday and Speller sat on the sideline waiting for Baxter to complete his plans with the reporter and photographer, Buck's little four-year-old daughter came over and stood in front of Friday. She looked up at him with her big brown eyes and asked, "What kind of hunk are you?"

At first, Friday wasn't sure that he'd heard right. "Did you say hunk?" he asked.

"Yes!" She planted her feet and put her hands on her hips. "Hunk."

"Well, I guess you might say I'm a hunk of clay."

Her eyes grew larger. Turning to where three young girls sat nearby, she yelled so all could hear, "He's a hunk of clay."

Everyone within hearing distance roared with laughter.

"So, you're a hunk of clay?" Speller turned to him, his eyes openly amused, and he said, "A number of years ago, I heard a song one of the country singers sang claiming he was nothing but a hunk of coal. That ought to let the girls know that you are different and original."

Speller's teasing laughter put Friday more at ease. When Buck heard the commotion, he came over to see what it was all about.

"I hope Maria isn't bothering you. She is a handful," he said apologetically, smiling at his daughter knowingly.

"Not at all. She just has an inquiring mind."

Buck walked off, shaking his head as he took his daughter by her hand and headed toward his wife.

Their work completed, Hallway and Baxter joined Friday and Speller.

What does it take to get a drink around here?" Baxter barked.

"We have a strict rule here. No alcohol on the premises," Hallway informed him.

"Guess that's a good idea, especially with the youngsters around." Turning to Speller, he asked, "Are you ready to leave?"

"Ready when you are."

Before they left, Baxter looked at Friday and said, "Speller tells me you're doing a good job. Look for the humor in things, boy; you'll have a lot more fun."

As an afterthought, before they reached the door, Friday picked up a bottle of Big Red, the favorite drink with this group of Hispanics, handed it to Baxter, and said, "Here—there's enough sugar in one of these babies to tie on a high."

Baxter and Speller laughed.

Friday noticed that Speller seemed ten years younger just then.

Who would have thought one could have such an enjoyable evening without one drop of alcohol?

Friday looked forward to the next social that would take place in two weeks. As for Speller, he was glad he got the chance to know Friday better during this strange encounter.

The following Monday, when it was time to get back to work, Friday overheard the men discussing what happened Saturday. For the rest of his stay, he was referred to, jokingly, as the "hunk."

□□□□□

It was the third week of Friday's stay. Things were going well, that is, until he got in from the field to clean up before dinner and found a woman in his bed.

That occurrence made the month truly memorable.

She didn't speak English, but it didn't take Friday long to realize that she was in labor.

Between moans, she kept repeating something that didn't sound like Spanish or English.

Finally, she just kept repeating, "José, José," and Friday realized she wanted one of the men staying in the bunkhouse.

Friday ran to the bunkhouse to find José and to get help.

"That must be Metilda. José took the last load of vegetables to the cannery, and he isn't back," one of the men informed him.

"Get Rosie and her daughter; she'll know what to do," another man suggested.

Fortunately, Rosie and her daughter, Avelia, were still in the kitchen when Friday told them what was happening.

Rosie immediately took charge and told Avelia to call the midwife, Laura, and tell her to come immediately.

Rosie followed Friday back to his cabin. Assessing the situation, she asked Friday to stay and see that Metilda didn't fall off the bed.

When Avelia arrived at the cabin, Rosie sent her for towels and a basin of warm water to prepare for the delivery.

Metilda's moaning became more disturbing to Friday. He felt so helpless he just wanted to get out of there, but Rosie insisted that he stay. "We need your help," she said. "Just hold her hand until Laura gets here."

Friday did as he was told, but his mind locked onto the delivery room scene in the movie *Jersey Girl*. Ben Affleck was holding his wife's hand; the role played by Jennifer Lopez. The doctor in attendance directed Jennifer to take long, deep breaths, then push.

Friday took up the rhythm and encouraged Metilda to do likewise.

He became oblivious to his surroundings and so caught up in the moment it took the sound of a slap and the husky cry of the baby to bring Friday out of his state of concentration.

The door opened, and Laura appeared with her bag, prepared to take over. José was behind her.

Laura looked surprised to see a man standing beside the bed.

"You didn't need me; it seems," she said with a grin as she surveyed Friday.

José came to the bedside, and Friday took the opportunity to get out, stumbling for the bunkhouse. He was mentally exhausted. She had been in labor for over six hours.

It was after midnight, and the men there were still awake and excited to hear what had happened. Friday told them, "I helped Metilda until the midwife came," and he fell into a bed.

"What is Buck going to do when he hears about this?" They all chorused.

Someone else asked, "Do you think he will fire José?"

As they discussed the situation, José walked in. "The women want me out of the room," he grinned and added, "I'm a papi." Everyone offered their congratulations.

José smiled and shrugged. His voice held a note of hopefulness. "I don't think Buck will fire me for letting this happen. It all happened so fast. Metilda wants all of our family to be Americans. She told me she would have this baby here, so it would be a U.S. citizen. I didn't think she meant here on the farm."

Another of the men suggested, "Maybe Buck doesn't have to know."

"Yeah," still another chimed in. "But what about Friday? Do you think he'll tell Buck?"

As they talked, they looked over at Friday, who had been trying to coax his body to sleep, but half-listening, he finally spoke up.

He said in Spanish, "No problem, José. Call the baby Buck and then ask Buck to be his godfather."

The suggestion struck them as the best solution. The lights went out shortly after one in the morning.

The next morning, José approached Friday and asked if he would mind having his picture taken with Metilda, his son, Rosie, and Avelia. "It will mean so much to Metilda," he said shyly.

As Friday stood smiling with them, he thought *guess I'll now be able to add delivery service to my resume.*

A Man Called Friday

Friday wasn't present when José told Buck what happened that night. Buck never brought up the subject, and neither did Friday. After all, such events were not so unusual. And Friday learned that midwives make a good living on the border.

Friday appended his final report before mailing it off to Speller.

"Well, I got my bed back the next morning, with a week to go before the month is up. I heard Metilda went back to Mexico with her little Buckaroo, just one more U. S. citizen living south of the border."

◻◻◻◻◻

He had a memorable learning experience, getting to know Buck, the pickers, and especially the home-cooked Tex-Mex food. He never did get to eat any of the oranges that Buck promised in his letter. The harvest of oranges wouldn't begin for another two weeks.

He added some personal comments to the report. "I'm glad I had the opportunity to live among the people who are responsible for planting, tending, and picking our food supply. It's not a profession I would choose to pursue for a livelihood. But I did notice something. The workers were proud, appreciative and all displayed an upbeat attitude. I'm certain Buck had something to do with their morale."

◻◻◻◻◻

Speller was more than pleased with Friday's report. It went into more depth than he expected. Friday had collected information regarding Buck's immediate family and about when he met Buck's wife and children.

Photos were also included. Any additional information Speller would elaborate upon when he wrote his version of the story.

He was in his office rereading the information and waiting to discuss the next assignment when Beth announced Friday's arrival.

OLIVIA ROUNDTREE

"Good to see you," Speller said with a smile. "I was just going over your report about Buck. And I think we have our next winner. He handed Friday a neatly typewritten letter.

Olivia Roundtree
1232 Bond Rd.
Mountain Ridge, N.D. 65481

Dear Sir:
SOS—Save Olivia's Sanity. I'm a fifty-two-year-old Spanish teacher. I don't do drugs, smoke, or drink, but I am a frustrated foodaholic. My problem: the three story house I inherited from my grandparents is packed and stacked with trash and treasures. A sixty by eighty-foot metal building that I intend to use, as my studio is also full of "crapola." Mice and moisture have taken their toll. I confess that I'm a pack rat—just can't throw anything away. The solution is Friday: He has my permission to sell, burn or bury this burden. I repeat, SOS.
Olivia

☐☐☐☐☐

"Well, what do you think?" Speller asked.

"I'm wondering if she really will let me make decisions about what she should discard or what she should keep," Friday replied. "What else did Beth find out about her?"

"School is out for the summer, so she will be home all day. She has authored a number of books and is published. You can leave next week—or do you need more time to regroup?" Speller asked.

"I'm doing fine," Friday replied. "Are all of the arrangements completed?"

"All except a definite beginning date," Speller said. "You can arrange that with Beth before you leave. Olivia will pick you up at the airport. Why don't you give her a call now? She can fill you in on the details." Speller handed Friday the phone.

Friday liked the idea and dialed the number to make his first contact. When Olivia answered, they chatted for several minutes.

After he hung up, Friday said, "She lives in North Dakota, another state that I know little about. I know that South Dakota is where Mount Rushmore and the Black Hills are, but I know nothing of the attractions in North Dakota. Wonder how far Mountain Ridge is from the Black Hills."

He paused and let his thoughts of Olivia ricochet through his mind like pinballs off a bumper. *Spanish teacher, hmmm, maybe the time I spent in South Texas with Buck will help."*

☐☐☐☐☐

The landing in North Dakota was smooth, and Friday looked forward to meeting Olivia Roundtree. He had been especially impressed when he found out that she was a writer and a teacher; she also wrote music and played the guitar and piano.

And he had to grin as he recalled what she said when he asked her on the phone how she would recognize him.

"Not to worry," she replied. "I've already painted a picture of you mentally, and I will recognize you."

Was she kidding, or did she have psychic abilities?

Standing at the luggage carousel, he scanned the room, eyeing all the females milling around.

Suddenly, he felt a nudge on his shoulder. "Friday! You must be the man who was sent by my ancestors to save my sanity."

He liked her immediately. She was a big woman, structured to an Amazonian scale. Right away, Friday noticed that her ancestry was probably Native American. Her long dark hair hung down her back to her waist; her face was striking with prominent cheekbones and a wide jaw, which triangulated into a firm chin. Her mouth was full, and her eyes were as clear as a blue sky, sparkling just a little bit, probably with the anticipation of Friday's arrival.

The talking they did on the drive to her twenty acres on the edge of town clued Friday in that she was a warm, caring person as she spoke about the students and the community where she was born, raised, and lived in all of her life.

Their destination was a well-kept farmhouse, which stood a hundred feet back from a dead-end road. It was of no particular architectural style, just a plain but cozy-looking three-story structure with blue siding, a brown shingle roof, and a wrap-around front porch.

Friday stopped in his tracks when he saw the statue of Quan Yin, the goddess of mercy, planted in the side yard surrounded by lush green ground cover. Three times in a period of two months, that statue had come to his attention—first on Speller's patio, then the one his mother had, and now this.

Could it be a coincidence?

"Does Quan Yin have significance for you?" he asked Olivia.

"Yes. Funny you should mention that. My father sent it to my mother. He was a correspondent for the New York Times and did a lot of foreign travel. My parents met and were married in New York. After he was killed in Viet Nam, mother moved us here to North Dakota, and four months later, this statue was delivered to her. The note taped on the back of the statue read, 'My spirit is inside this lady. I will always be near to protect you.' My mother assumed that Dad had purchased it before he was killed, and it was delayed in being delivered."

Interesting. Friday made a mental note to ask Speller if there was a story behind his statue of Quan Yin.

The second story of Olivia's house also had a wrap-around balcony, but it was the third story that caught Friday's attention.

It resembled a lighthouse tower with windows on all four sides.

Before he could open his mouth to ask about it, Olive began explaining. "The third story was my granddad's idea. He was a sea captain before he settled here to be near my grandmother's family. The back of the nest, as he called it, looks out over the lake. He would spend hours up there just sitting in a rocking chair playing his flute."

"As a child, my brother and I would sit at his feet while he told stories about growing up in Norway. I remembered them and wrote a trilogy about Norwegian children. It was published a number of years ago."

Noticing the painted scene of trees, birds, and flowers on one side of the attached garage, Friday asked, "And you're an artist, too?"

"Yes and no. I enjoy painting more as a hobby. This was done one weekend when I was frustrated, and my painting outlet surfaced. My friend, Trish, is the artist. She helped me. You'll meet her while you're here. In fact, a number of my friends are looking forward to meeting you."

Olivia recalled the day she told her two friends, Trish and Frieda, about the letter she wrote to the radio station that was sponsoring a contest offering A Man Called Friday. They were in the teacher's lounge after lunch.

"For a whole month, he will be at my side to help me finally get rid of all the crapola that I've been wanting to discard for years. I know you gals volunteered to help me, but it's a man's job," Olivia explained.

"What did you write?" Trish asked, intrigued by the idea.

Before Olivia could reply, Frieda voiced her opinion, "You can bet it was off the wall."

"Not really." Olivia grinned. "When I heard the announcement on the radio, it got my attention. I began remembering all the stuff the kids left behind when they began their new life away from Mom. Now seems to be the right time to get rid of it. I'll just let Friday do it."

"Hey, you sound like it's already a done deal that you'll win," Frieda quipped.

"Maybe I am jumping the gun, but I've already made a list of things that need to be burned, buried, or sold at a yard sale," Olivia said as her dark eyebrows arched mischievously.

"Tell us what you wrote," Trish encouraged.

"This is not verbatim, but it went something like this: SOS Save Olivia's Sanity—then I admitted I was a pack rat and that I would give permission for Friday to help me sort things out—like give it to Goodwill, maybe have a yard sale, or just burn most of it."

"I just know you're going to win." Trish patted Olivia on the shoulder as they walked out of the teacher's lounge to their classrooms.

And she had won.

☐☐☐☐☐

"I'll give you the Realtor's Tour," Olivia announced as they walked toward the front porch. "So today, we will use the front door."

"Enter!" With flair, she bowed and extended her hand—like the models do on The Price is Right for displaying merchandise.

"The Social Gathering Room, where I feed and water my friends, where my writer peers meet for critiquing sessions. And when I'm in the mood to have a sit-down meal instead of eating in the office or in front of the TV."

"Wow!" was Friday's only comment as he stood assessing the room and its contents: deep pink walls with a round table and chairs in the center of the room, and throughout the remainder of the space, there were shelves, pictures, and small tables crammed with figurines, knick-knacks, trinkets. It reminded him of the antique shop and tearoom he frequented with his former wife. He referred to the collector's items as dust catchers, and he was glad that his ex took them with her when she left.

I'll bet that each one of these dust catchers has a sentimental attachment. I had best forget even suggesting that she part with any of this stuff.

Taking it all in, he made no comment as he followed her into the next room—the living room. He was surprised. It wasn't cluttered. In fact, it was sparsely furnished. The room had a feeling of permanence and continuity. It exuded constancy and stability compared to the first room, perhaps as a reaction to Olivia's having lost her mother when she was only fifteen.

This woman had to be a Gemini. They exhibited several personalities. Friday's friend, Jed, had explained that a Gemini is someone born between May 21st and June 20th, someone who could exhibit characteristics of several personalities. Jed was married to one, and he was always sharing the off-the-wall things she did and the ideas she had.

Friday would ask Olivia later when her birthday was.

"It's like being married to two women," Jed told Friday.

Only a television, stereo, rocking chair, an oversized low table, and a comfortable couch up against one wall were in this room.

On the pale blue walls, the paintings of seascapes, boats, and still lifes showed outstanding talent. They hung on all four walls. He paused to study the seascape that looked so real he wanted to touch it to see if it was moist.

"Yours?" he asked.

"My mother's," she answered. "This is my Feel-Good Room, where my mother and grandparents gathered after church on Sundays. My grandmother read passages from the Bible, and we had discussions. At that time, I had no idea that my mother was so seriously ill. She had heart trouble and did a lot of resting and painting."

Olivia closed her eyes for a moment, trying to keep the memory pure and unsullied. Abruptly, she opened her eyes and returned to reality. "The seascape is the last painting she did."

Opening another door, she led Friday into her office. "And this is my Inspiration Room. I do all my writing here."

The walls were lined with books on every subject. There was a huge mahogany desk with a computer and printer-copier against one wall. In the corner by the window was a comfortable overstuffed recliner.

"Many a morning, I wake up in this chair when I'm doing rewrites for a deadline," she explained.

"Do you name all your rooms?" Friday asked.

Olivia laughed. "Now that you mention it, I guess I do. See the door beside the file cabinet? That's the Throne Room. Guess you don't need an explanation as to what's in there."

Olivia was enjoying sharing her home and possessions with Friday.

"Everyone that plays a musical instrument should have a Music Room," she said as she opened the door between two bookcases.

That's when Friday shook his head as he looked around and saw the grand piano, drum sets, guitars, and music stands.

"Twice a month, my friends meet here to practice. We play at local functions. There are seven regulars. We play country-western. Several of us write music, and we have a blast experimenting with new songs. Do you play?" she asked, turning to Friday.

"Drums, as a teenager, but that was a long time ago."

"We will see about that," she said and looked at him as a thoughtful smile curved her mouth.

"And yes, the place comes with a kitchen. You will always find popcorn on the cabinet to graze on. It quells my hunger. A hand full tides me over from pigging out on sweets." She giggled like a teenager.

"The cooking is not gourmet," she admitted. "I'm addicted to fast food, and my ample body testifies that I tend to overdo it. Off the kitchen is my bedroom, which is not open to the public. Bed unmade, clothes on the chair—get the picture? Let's go upstairs where you will be staying."

The second story had four bedrooms and at the end of the hall was a spacious bathroom.

"Prepare yourself," she warned as she led Friday up the stairs.

The first room was definitely feminine. "My daughter's room. She is living in Florida with her husband and daughter. I never did clear out all her stuff. She told me she doesn't want anything in here and to do with it as I please."

There were two love seats, three chests of drawers, a full bed, and cardboard boxes stacked to the ceiling against one wall. The closet door was open, and the closet itself was packed with clothes. "She had intentions of covering the soiled love seats but never did. They've definitely got to go."

Yeah, Friday thought, definitely fire pile material.

They walked to the second door; the odor of sweaty tennis shoes that were beside the bed and dirty clothes stacked in chairs irritated Friday's nose. He let out a violent sneeze when Olivia opened the door.

"Let's open some windows to let out this musty odor," she suggested.

More chairs that needed repair, a card table, and two single beds. Definitely not my choice of a room I would want to sleep in.

"My son's room, not the neatest kid, as you can see. I haven't been in his room in over a year. He is a traveling musician. Last time I heard from him, he was in England. Sorry about this mess. Let's move on."

The third room they entered was livable. It was stacked with collapsible chairs; the bed looked comfortable. A huge window definitely could use some Windex, but it looked out over the countryside.

"The bedding is in the downstairs washroom, and you can get it later. I'm sorry about not having things prepared, but I've been so busy at school I am exhausted at night when I get home." Her tone was apologetic.

"That's okay. That's my job while I'm here—to make your life more comfortable and easier," Friday assured her.

The fourth room looked like a used furniture store. A lot of the stuff was broken, waiting to be fixed or glued together, or if not worth the effort, to be on the burn pile—a broken window that needed a new pane. Friday could see he had his work cut out for him.

"In your letter, you mentioned that you had a storage room and that you had accumulated a lot of trash and treasures. Is that the building out there?" Friday looked out of the window where there were several small sheds and one large metal building.

"We can get to that tomorrow. I hate to turn you off on your first day. You might just pack up and be gone by morning if you see what's in there. Oh! In case you want to explore my granddad's nest, you can get to it by the door at the end of the hall. It opens to the outside balcony, and the stairs go up to the nest," she explained.

Olivia had a feeling that he definitely was interested in that room.

"Let's go back downstairs. I picked up some sandwiches from the deli. I hope you like champagne, compliments of Trish. 'Welcome him with a little bubbly.' Trish is a character, as I'm sure you will agree when you meet her. Now I want to hear all about you," Olivia said as they headed for the stairs.

They ate the sandwiches and drank champagne in the Social Gathering Room while they became better acquainted.

They had been discussing Friday's adventures while he was at the vegetable farm with Buck and his month's stay with the Skylarks in Tennessee. Olivia was familiar with the people and area where Buck lived. She had spent one summer in South Texas.

When she heard the word Skylark, she recognized the name.

"Skylark! That name rings a bell. Did they entertain on a cruise ship?"

"As a matter of fact, they did," Friday said, a look of surprise on his face.

"One of the teachers went on a cruise several summers ago, and she came home raving about the Skylark's performances. She said it was the highlight of the cruise."

"Well, I had a ringside seat. I know what she was talking about. They were fantastic." Friday saw no need to go into the tragic details of May's illness. "Before I left, Faye gave me three tapes that were made available at their performances. I haven't had time to listen to them yet. I left them with Speller to listen to."

They were exchanging stories like a family would when one of the family members returned after a trip. One can lose all track of time, which is what had happened. Olivia was so easy to talk to.

Suddenly, Olivia looked at the clock and exclaimed, "I can't believe it's after 2:00 a.m.! We'd better call it a night. It's been a long day for you," as she pulled away from the table to get up.

Before she left to go to her room, she reminded Friday that the kitchen was a do-it-yourself place. "Get up when you feel like it. Coffee and muffins are on the counter. I will make no promises when I will be up. The sheds and building are open if you want to explore."

Friday made up his bed, choosing the third room, to make it his quarters for the next month. He mentally decided what he would take out and how he would arrange it to his liking as he got ready to go to bed.

As soon as his head hit the pillow, he was asleep.

It was shortly after 3:00 a.m. when he awoke to the sound of flute music. He opened his eyes for a moment, looking to see if there was a radio in the room that he might have overlooked.

No radio.

Olivia, he decided, must be listening to a tape. Turning over, he went back to sleep.

☐☐☐☐☐

Birds were chirping outside and the sun flooding the room with light enticed Friday to get up and begin the new day. He was anxious to see all of the trash and treasures that Olivia had accumulated over the years. Would he find a treasure?

He felt like a kid on Christmas morning. This was going to be fun. After taking a shower, he slipped on a pair of khaki shorts and a polo shirt.

The house was quiet when he entered the kitchen and flipped on the two-cup Mr. Coffee. He buttered a fruit bran muffin and took his coffee mug and muffin out onto the patio.

The sparrows and redbirds were fighting for space at the feeder, wings flapping, shoving each other from the curved perches.

They scattered when Friday pulled up a chair.

In a nearby oak, two squirrels ignored him as they scampered from limb to limb, playing catch me if you can.

As he watched, Friday gave a sigh of contentment. What a beautiful, peaceful day.

Finishing his breakfast, Friday headed for the metal building. He raised the handle on the door and stepped back, envisioning piles of junk.

He was relieved that the boxes were neatly arranged around the sides. The center of the wooden floor held an assortment of furniture, some of which looked to be in good shape. Might as well try to sell some of this stuff, and what didn't sell, he could haul off to Goodwill.

He pulled out his notebook to make a list of things to discuss with Olivia so she could make the final decision concerning what to discard or keep.

Books, books, and more books were in the first five boxes he opened. Mostly paperbacks, enough to start a library. A computer and printer, probably needing repair, sat on top of a stack of boxes. He was just getting ready to take them down when he heard a car drive up. He stepped outside the building to investigate.

"Morning, I'm Paul, Olivia's friend," a pudgy-faced man with horn-rimmed glasses yelled out the window of the station wagon.

Friday walked over to the car to greet him.

"Olivia told me that you might stop by to lend me a hand. I'm just getting started, and, as you can see, there must be almost a hundred boxes. So far, all I've opened have contained books."

"Did you notice the dates written on top of each box?" Paul asked. "Those boxes contain paper records for each year she taught. She is sentimental, and her students' work is very important, especially if they wrote promising essays," Paul explained.

"Let's sit on the patio, and I'll fix us a cup of coffee until Olivia joins us," Friday suggested.

As they sat and drank their coffee, Friday said, "Olivia tells me that you are an airline pilot, and you play the piano in her band."

71

"That's correct. I've known Olivia for ten years. My daughter was one of her students. She and my wife, now my ex, were good friends. But that's in the past. My wife and daughter are now living in Spain. Two years ago, my daughter spent a year as an exchange student in Spain, and my wife went to visit her for a month. While there, my ex met her soulmate, and the rest is history. To date, I haven't found my soulmate, and I'm still looking." Paul grinned as he waited for Friday's reaction.

Before Friday could respond, Olivia popped her head out from the patio door and joined them.

"I see you met our Jerry Lee Lewis," Olivia said mischievously. "When you hear Paul play the piano tomorrow night, you'll see what I'm talking about."

Turning to Paul, she asked, "You will be joining us, won't you? I can never keep up with your schedule."

"I'll be here. And I'll be here to join the group for that Newcomers luncheon Trish booked for us."

After listening to the conversation between Paul and Olivia, Friday began to study them the way Ray and Faye taught him to observe, to truly get to know them.

In his judgment, Paul was as emotionally stable as the Rock of Gibraltar and as easy going as a golden retriever on Valium, which was probably why Olivia just smiled at him while he chattered on.

She appeared reluctant to take him seriously. It was obvious to Friday that Paul had deeper feelings for Olivia than mere friendship. Paul was definitely a C-C-D, Caring Cool Dude, and Olivia was a T-F, Tutti-Fruity. Friday often used initials to tag people since being let in on Ray Skylark's secret. This was his private joke for now.

From the routine dull life of an accountant to the arena full of snap, crackle, and pop people, he was having the time of his life.

It was after 10:00 a.m. when Friday stood up and announced, "To work, to work."

For the remainder of the day, they sorted out boxes for the burn pile and what would go to Goodwill. Friday was surprised when Olivia looked at the dates on the boxes briefly, sorted through the contents, and declared, "This can go."

Friday knew she must be a very popular and well-liked teacher. So many of the boxes held gifts from her students. It's-the-thought-that-counts types of gifts, cups, miniature statues—all were set aside and would be donated to Goodwill to be recycled.

Olivia called it a day after 6:00 p.m. Before Paul left, he suggested that they meet at a German Pub at eight. "We'll eat, drink and be merry," he said as he left to get into his car.

It had been a long time since Friday enjoyed himself as much as he did that evening. Paul rounded up the band members to join the threesome.

Friday learned that Trish, Freda, Betsy, Tom, and Don were all teachers.

Betsy read his palm; Freda and Trish added up his birth numbers to do numerology, and he was told his life path was a five, the number of The Adventurer.

Betsy was also an astrologer. "Just a hobby," she told him.

All Friday knew about the subject was what he read in the Daily Globe newspaper. He occasionally would read it, not that he believed in any of that generalized daily forecast, but sometimes the stuff was interesting.

Born on May 29th, he was a Gemini, and he learned that Olivia was also a Gemini. He couldn't personally relate to the characters that Gemini people had in common.

"Friday, no wonder you are a great helper. Your Mercury is in Virgo," Betsy declared.

"How about a late bloomer," Trish added in a joking way. Trish was definitely an S-S-S, Serious-Silly-Sermonish.

A subject that Friday was not too familiar with was the Chinese Horoscope. He knew from reading the paper place mats in the Chinese restaurants that he was a Rat.

"Oh my God! We have two Super Duper Rats in our midst," Freda shouted.

"How did you come up with that?" Friday asked.

"It's your sun sign and animal sign combined," Freda explained. "It means that both you and Olivia are always one step ahead of the pack. I can't believe you and Olivia are both Gold Gemini Rats."

Friday learned that Olivia was twelve years older than he was and that, as a five Life Path, it was his destiny to travel extensively. It also indicated that he had a vivid imagination and would excel as a writer. In fact, in his harvest cycle, starting at age fifty-six, he would begin writing full-time.

He didn't share his 'compulsive disorder' about making lists and taking notes on everything he observed, heard, or experienced. Maybe he could share that later. But writing and being a published author, he couldn't buy. Taking notes and making lists didn't make him a Brown, Grisham, Clancy, or Koontz.

They were recognized for their talent by the major newspapers and sold millions of books. He was being made fun of by his peer group. As a L-N-T, List-Note-Taker, he decided that P-W, People Watcher, was his persona.

Friday learned so much more about himself that night; it got him thinking. Now, he was not only an L-N-T and a P-W; he was becoming more aware of the occult. He asked himself, where have I been all these years and not aware? Or is my interest heightened by the people I am now coming into contact with?

Perhaps he did miss out on important moments of his life. Olivia had referred to a quote from Helene Keller several times since they met, and she said it again now, "Life is either a daring adventure or nothing."

He was surprised when Paul put in his two cents worth. "What Olivia is trying to tell you is for you to make the rest of your life the best of your life. She tells me that all the time, too." Paul grinned and added, "Sounds like a Hallmark moment, doesn't it?"

☐☐☐☐☐

OLIVIA ROUNDTREE

As Friday pondered Olivia and Paul's comments, he wondered if he was being silly or cynical. He wasn't sure. Before he finally went to sleep that night, he felt comforted by the most amazing sense of belonging.

He had an overwhelming feeling that something of monumental importance was about to happen to him. He could feel cold chills run up and down his back.

It was 3:00 a.m. when Friday awoke to the mellow notes of a flute drifting softly through the room. Spellbound by the enchanting music, he felt he was not alone. Then he opened his eyes and saw a small white-bearded man wearing a white robe standing at the foot of his bed.

"Who are you?" Friday asked, a little alarmed.

"I'm a member of the White Brotherhood."

"Why are you here?"

"To remind you why you came to planet earth in a physical body."

"I'm sorry. I'm confused. Is Olivia playing a prank on me?"

"Olivia would never do such a thing. I am your guide. Some refer to me as an angel, others a messenger.

"In the past, I have contacted you in a dream state. Periodically, I appear to check up on your progress. Most mortals are not able to see in the spiritual dimension where I reside. But, as the evolutionary process on planet earth continues, more mortals will be able to see into other dimensions.

"Be assured you are not hallucinating or dreaming. I am here with you now. I would never impose my concepts for decisions you are faced with. You will always have free will to make your own choices and mistakes," the old man explained patiently.

"Tonight, you were given a lot to think about by your newfound friends. It is no accident that you are now among them, although at this time you do not remember, you have been together many times in the past. I'm here to enlighten you.

"When one becomes restless and dissatisfied with their present situation, it's time to venture on, as you have done when you accepted this opportunity to meet total strangers and assist them in making their responsibilities more pleasant—a wise decision, I might add." He paused, then added, "A major stepping-up process with your mission is about to begin."

"How will I know what my mission is and if I am following it? My reason for being?" Friday wanted to know.

"That is why I am here to let you know you are on track. No one is ever abandoned; there are always guides that come periodically to observe your progress. Also, there is a definite conformation you experience when what you see, or hear, is truth. You feel cold chills run down your back. Have you ever had that sensation?"

"Why yes, many times, but I was not aware that it had any significance."

"Now you know. In the future, you will be able to take comfort that you are following your mission."

Friday was awestruck. Was this a dream, or was there actually a man in the room with him? He felt he was awake while having this conversation. The answers made sense.

"Will I be able to see you again and communicate as we are doing?"

The old man smiled and replied, "I'm on duty twenty-four, seven. I, too, am learning something by being around the younger generation.

"You are never alone. If I am not here, someone else will be. There is another way that you should become aware of. When you are at a social gathering or many times having a one-to-one conversation, look into the eyes of that person. The eyes are the mirrors of the soul. When you see transformation in their facial features, this will be indicative that they are responding from past experiences or that someone is using their body temporarily to convey choices you might want to consider.

"You have had numerous opportunities to witness this. The time spent with Speller, the Skylarks, Buck, and now Olivia, Trish, and everyone that you have met in the past. And from this day forward, the people you meet are there for your learning experiences."

"What am I supposed to learn from all of this? I confess this is all new to me." Friday's interest deepened as he spoke with the old man.

"You are here to help make this planet a better place for the ones that follow. There are other star systems, planets, and galaxies with life that a finite mind cannot comprehend at this time. Planet Earth is a classroom for learning, experiencing, and overcoming. You might consider it a place for the "grow as you go" plan toward more spiritual awareness and to discover who you truly are. A spiritual being in a physical body."

With that explanation, the old man faded away.

Friday sat up in bed, looking around the room. The bedside clock displayed the time—3:15 a.m. Friday waited, then turned over and went back to sleep.

The sun and bird sounds woke Friday shortly after 7:00 a.m. Before going downstairs, he decided to explore the third-story nest.

The door was unlocked. As he stepped into the eight-by-ten glass-walled room, the three-hundred-sixty-degree picturesque scene of treetops, lush green fields of clover, and the Crystal Lake created a feeling of such beauty he felt awestruck. The room was sparsely furnished with only an oversized maple rocker and a small table beside it with a flute on top. On the wooden floor was a round, blue braided rug.

Olivia had told him that her granddad played the flute, but why was it still here? She said he had died years ago.

He seated himself in the rocking chair and was momentarily tempted to play the flute as he examined it when something happened that was foreign to the logical, realistic Friday. He thought he heard someone say, "Only humans, cursed with the knowledge of their own mortality and that of those they loved, are truly alone; each trapped in an ivory tower of skull and bone peeking out through the windows of the soul."

Friday turned around to see if last night's visitor was there.

No one.

Suddenly his attention was drawn to a blue jay perched on the window ledge in front of him. It stood large and polished and looked royally remote.

There were no other birds in the area.

A feeling of joy overwhelmed Friday. The bird stood enormous, looking at him. Abruptly, it turned, revealing the black bars across its wings and tail.

As Friday watched, he thought he'd somehow only now learned how to see. He had never seen anything so clearly, and it was not simply because the jay was posted where it was, close enough for him to note the details and vibrant color. It seemed like he was seeing things in a different light.

A feeling that mere words could not describe flooded over him, and tears of gratitude ran down his cheeks.

What just happened?

He wiped the tears from his face. Again, he experienced blissful peace and contentment. No wonder Olivia's granddad spent so much time in the nest.

What was happening to him? Friday wondered as he cleared his throat and stood up, ready for breakfast.

Olivia was making coffee when Friday entered the kitchen. "Hope you like Spanish omelets," she said in greeting.

They took their plates out to the patio, and after eating, they sat sipping their coffee, drifting in and out of lazy conversation.

Suddenly, Friday could no longer contain his curiosity about the nest. He wanted to learn more about her grandfather. He told her what he had experienced as he sat in the rocker about seeing the bird so clearly.

"For a moment, I felt like I became the bird," he said.

He didn't tell her about the 3:00 a.m. visitor. He had to give it some more serious thought before he would discuss it with anyone.

"You had an epiphany," Olivia said in a matter-of-fact tone. She didn't bother to elaborate but began telling Friday about her son, Rick. She told him how he found the nest to be one of his favorite places to hide out while he was growing up and that he, too, played the flute as well as the guitar.

"And I'm sure he had a number of epiphanies. The nest seems to help us connect to our soul level," she explained. "Rick composed music for his band while he was in high school. I know the flute is still on the table waiting for him to come home for one of his rare visits—and to leave abruptly when he becomes restless.

"As for you hearing a flute—I believe you because I hear it too. It can be explained in one of two ways. One way is that you and I have vivid imaginations based on the fact that I know that my granddad enjoyed playing it, and I told you that he played the flute.

"The second explanation, although definitely not logical, would be that my granddad makes frequent visits to his nest to remind us that he is still around. So do you have another explanation?" she asked, assessing Friday before she continued discussing metaphysical issues.

For several moments, there was an awkward silence.

Finally, Friday broke the silence. "Hearing music that doesn't come from a radio and comes in the middle of the night is spooky."

Olivia was glad she hadn't continued the conversation on that subject. Since she could not only hear music, she could see spirits, she could communicate with them and many times read people's minds and tell them things she saw in their futures.

Perhaps when she knew him better, she would tell Friday more about her experiences that definitely were not of this dimension.

Spooky, he said. That's mild. What she could tell him might just scare the "yell" out of him. She knew that he was not ready for more. She didn't want to be known as a psychic and to make him uncomfortable. Besides, psychics were not all-knowing, as some of the movies would lead you to believe.

Changing the subject, they began discussing plans for a three-day yard sale to dispose of the still usable furniture. Today, Friday would begin to burn the boxes and contents from the metal building.

The entire day was spent sorting. They had separated out what to sell and what to burn. After a short dinner break, Friday made a fire pit and started a small fire. He invited Olivia to start throwing things into the flames., which grew into a bonfire in short order. She enjoyed the ritual of offering her old papers to the fire as a metaphor for releasing her past and moving forward. Her relief at letting go of it all created a feeling of lightness in her, which was contagious, and by the end of the night, she and Friday were positively buoyant.

The following day was spent carrying down items from upstairs to add to the sale and finding more useless items to be burned.

Friday felt comfortable listing the items and getting Olivia's suggestions as to their disposal. She left Friday pretty much to himself as she spent most of the day in her office writing.

She meant what she said that she did little cooking. She always had take-out for their evening meals. Lunch was generally fruit, energy bars, and juice. And thank God for the ever-present bowl of popcorn.

The first week went by smoothly, with a great deal accomplished.

Paul stopped by for coffee on several occasions during the evening.

Friday's next project would be the two small storage sheds. Olivia told him that they contained frames, canvases, painting supplies, and some of the work of her students and friends.

"It's going to be tough to decide what to keep," she told him. Her grandmother had died just ten months ago, and Olivia had put some of her things in the shed to sort out later but couldn't bring herself to accomplish the task until now.

That evening as they sat on the patio, Olivia shared her goals and plans with Friday. She told him that when she retired from teaching in public school, she wanted to use the metal building as an Art-Writing Studio, a place to teach and encourage gifted children.

She did volunteer work at one of the Indian reservations for a month each summer, and she saw the need to do something about helping them.

"I even envision building a dorm, nothing fancy, just a place for students to stay for a month in the summer. I've already done the math, and for this project, I will need at least two hundred thousand dollars. It won't be as fancy as Oprah's school in Africa, but the work will be just as important.

"I get goose bumps just thinking about it. It won't be difficult to find promising young people who display art and writing talent. To start out, it will be a summer art camp. Who knows, it may turn out to be a year-round project."

Pensively, she looked out into the dark and sighed.

"It sounds like you have been giving it some serious thought for some time," Friday said.

"If it's meant to be, the money will come, so I can carry out my plans. At the present time, I have saved about a fourth of what it will cost. But I have confidence that it will happen," she told him.

Friday was impressed with her positive attitude and confidence. He recalled the first day he started to clean out the metal building.

When he announced, "To work, to work," she grinned and said, "Whenever I'm faced with a situation that requires sweat and strain and pain, I look at it as an opportunity for beneficial physical therapy. Plus, I certainly can use more exercise."

Friday found himself relishing his accomplishments. Perhaps it was because Olivia kept complimenting him on his organizational skills and telling him how impressed she was with all that he had done in such a short time. Tomorrow she would be gone for the day at an out-of-town meeting.

The weather was great, and the early morning hours were especially pleasant as he sorted through the art supplies that were lined up on the shelves in the shed. Moisture and mice had destroyed most of the canvases. There were a lot of cans of dried-up paint and old picture frames too rotted to keep.

There was little to salvage except for one picture that had been covered with a blanket. It must have been stored recently because it was in good shape.

Friday stood admiring and studying the portrait of a white-bearded man pointing to an open book as a child looked over his shoulder.

Looking for the artist's signature on the painting, he found none. He turned it over, examining it more closely. Surely, someone with such talent would sign his or her name. He would ask Olivia what she knew about the painting when she returned.

But Olivia wasn't much help. All she recalled was that it was left to her by a distant cousin of her grandmother's in her will. It was mailed to her grandmother from Italy shortly before her death.

"I remember when it arrived, we were looking for a suitable place to hang it. It was leaning up against the wall in the living room, and grandmother died before we could hang it. I put it in the shed to get it out of the way until later. Guess I forgot it was there," Olivia explained.

"I think you have a masterpiece here. The only problem is I can't find the artist's signature. Would you mind if I did a little research on it? I know just the person who can help," Friday said.

"You're welcome to try, but who would know if there is no signature?" she asked.

"My partner's wife, Amanda, is an art teacher. She has made numerous trips abroad. I venture to say from our conversations that she has visited every art gallery in Europe. I'm certain she would be helpful. I'll give her a call."

Amanda was glad to hear from Friday. She would be pleased if she was able to help him in any way. She suggested that he email her a picture of the canvas.

When he told her that there was no signature, she informed him that some artists hid their signatures in their work. It was popular with some of the painters in the 17th century, especially Italian artists. You may have discovered a rare painting." She laughed.

When Friday relayed what Amanda said, Olivia squealed, erupting in sudden laughter. He then set about getting the photo to Amanda.

There was little sleeping in the house that night. Olivia was like a child anticipating her first trip to Disneyland.

The news came by phone the following morning during breakfast. Olivia answered the phone and handed it to Friday.

"I think your friend is the owner of a painting by a French artist." She suggested putting it on the Internet with an opening bid of $5,000, which Olivia did that same day.

The bidding quickly ignited a firestorm of bidding among French and American art lovers and galleries around the country. A private art collector finally won with a whopping final bid of $710,429! Olivia and Friday sat stunned as they watched the bids come in on the home computer.

Experts linked the work to an old master named Pier Francesco Mola.

Before the buyer sent one of his staff to collect the picture in person, Friday and Olivia kept looking for where the artist might have signed his name.

Olivia discovered it when she turned the painting upside down. It was so obvious from that perspective. It was signed in the old man's beard.

"I insist that you take this check as a finder's fee for making all this possible," Olivia demanded the day Friday left when his month was up. "I will not take no for an answer," she declared.

"You win," Friday finally relented as he took the check she offered. Signing his name on the back, he handed it back to her and said, "I want to make a donation to be set aside and used for scholarships for students that are in need of financial aid.

☐☐☐☐☐

Friday summed up his experience in his own words prior to writing his report.

"I can sum up my month's experience in six words—I learned to live—not just exist.

"Because Speller insists on more details, I will elaborate. After the second week, Olivia and I had a close relationship akin to a big sister and her little brother. She explained her personal ongoing research of self-awareness. Her favorite word is "discern." For everything, she told me about her personal experiences sounded more like science fiction, and I'll be discerning for a long time.

"Everything is possible, but the only way to accept something is to experience it for yourself. Don't try to prove anything; let them prove it to themselves. This is another food for thought suggestion I intend to practice."

"It was not all work, oops, I mean physical therapy for me during my month's stay. Trish, Paul, Olivia, and I went to South Dakota to view the Black Hills and Mount Rushmore."

"The band members talked me into playing the drums during the two sessions they met while I was there. I never again heard the flute playing after the first night. When I told Olivia about my experience with the blue bird in the nest, she just smiled and said, 'Come on, admit it, you had an epiphany. You're no threat to the nuns and priests. They experience epiphanies quite often.'"

"Yes, I did spend a lot of time in the nest. The blue bird never returned, nor did I see the man who claimed he was my guide. I sat and read the books Olivia authored.

"And one more thing I must share. Olivia does not believe in accidents, happenstances, luck, or coincidences. 'You set it up with your thinking,' she explains."

"This I now believe."

TRISH

As Friday walked toward the office complex where Speller was waiting for him, he questioned whether or not to tell Speller of his plans to return to North Dakota after his assignment was over.

He had a definite feeling that he would be seeing more of this close-knit group and wanted to continue the relationships, especially with Trish.

His thoughts filtered back to the day he first met Trish. She stopped by to drop off a book she borrowed from Olivia. When she walked in the door and saw Friday for the first time, she greeted him in a joking way.

"Olivia didn't tell me what a hunk you are."

"Yeah, that's me, a hunk of clay."

"Mind your manners, girl; I don't think he is used to our cutting up and our off-beat sense of humor." Olivia's eyes grew openly amused as she continued to voice her advice. "Give him time to find out that you are a rainbow of fruit flavors."

Trish looked at Friday and smiled a perfect smile. Their eyes lingered for a second, and Friday, glancing down, noticed that there was no wedding ring on her finger.

She was tall and a little too thin. Her hair was dark red and cut short and smart above the ears. Her eyes were light brown, very big and round, and quite pleasant to gaze into for a second or two.

She really was quite attractive.

Olivia and Trish were probably two of the most offbeat people he had ever met. They were fast friends in spite of all the ways they differed from each other. Both were artists, not by choice or inclination but by compulsion.

Olivia painted with words; Trish painted with paint, and they approached their different arts with identical high standards, commitment, and craftsmanship.

One evening, during his stay in North Dakota, Olivia announced that they were going to the library to attend the showing of one of Trish's murals that she had just completed.

"You must come with us," Olivia insisted, "she will be so pleased."

It turned out to be quite an affair. The mayor, city council, and a room full of business dignitaries, along with the entire teaching staff where Trish taught, were present for the occasion.

Friday learned that Trish had completed a number of murals in public buildings throughout the community and surrounding towns. He was impressed with her talent and anxious to see more of her work.

Trish smiled when she spotted Friday with Olivia. She was pleased and surprised when he approached her and asked if she would give him a tour of all the places where her other works were displayed.

While Trish and Friday were talking, Olivia came over, followed by two women, to where they were standing.

"Friday, I want you to meet Trish's mother, Myra, and her Aunt Martha. They have a German Pub on the outskirts of town. You are not leaving Round Rock until you have a taste of some of their authentic German cooking, especially their Halupki—'to die for'," she said, laughing.

"And just what is Halupki?" Friday asked.

"It's stuffed cabbage baked in tomato sauce and beer," Martha explained.

"And how about your crusty sourdough bread with melted cheese?" Olive encouraged. "I swear I can pack on the pounds just thinking about it."

Friday learned a lot about Trish that night on the way back home after they left the library.

Trish was married. Her son and husband were killed in a motorcycle accident two years earlier. It was such a devastating blow for Trish to recover.

"Trish and her family were so close," Olivia explained.

The second week of Friday's stay, Trish came by to pick him up and take him to the Pub for dinner at the invitation of Trish's Aunt Martha. Olivia was invited, too, but she declined saying she needed to work on a chapter deadline. Actually, she wanted to give Trish the opportunity to get to know Friday better.

She had noticed how Friday looked at Trish the first time they met and whenever she was around.

Olivia was more than aware that Trish missed the attention of a man and wanted her to get to know Friday better. Without being too obvious, she invited Trish over more often to join her for coffee or any excuse she could think of.

Then she would excuse herself and let the two of them spend time together.

Friday found himself looking forward to seeing Trish and their time alone. It only emphasized how ready he was for change. He liked having someone whose step fell in alongside his, some one person he could anticipate seeing walk through the door.

He discovered, to his surprise, that he was tired of being alone, if not lonely.

It was—gravitational between Trish and him.

One weekend, the four—Paul, Olivia, Trish, and Friday—went to review all the paintings Trish had done over the past ten years.

Friday took pictures of each of her works and insisted that she pose beside them. For some reason, he was so proud of her and wanted to share her work with Speller and his mother.

Strange! He thought.

"It's just a hobby I enjoy doing. Teaching is my first love," Trish explained when Friday complimented her on her talent.

And before he left for home, Friday vowed to learn more about soul mates, if indeed there was such a thing. Perhaps that was why he was so attracted to Trish.

A Man Called Friday

THOMAS BRADEN
NO COINCIDENCES

Speller was in quite a jolly mood when Beth announced Friday's arrival.

He got up from behind his desk and led Friday to the social area in the office, where a leather couch with two chairs surrounded a coffee table.

"Have a seat, young man. We need to celebrate. I am so pleased with what you have reported that I'm getting more enthused by the day." He patted Friday on the shoulder.

Once they were seated, Speller poured two cups of jasmine tea from an oriental teapot that was on the table, along with an array of appetizers. This was a celebration and an occasion for them to become better acquainted.

"I know from your reports that you had some rough challenges as well as some special and rewarding experiences. The detailed descriptions in your accounts are excellent. You are a talented writer," Speller proclaimed, his eyes glowing with excitement. "Have you given any thought to becoming a serious writer?" He picked up a small cracker with cheese on it and put it in his mouth, savoring it while eyeing Friday.

Friday started to laugh as he began telling him about his compulsive list and note-taking disorder. He continued by saying how he began carrying a notebook around, imitating his stepdad, who was a detective and obsessed with details.

"That's been the extent of my writing," he explained. "I've never given any serious thought to writing as a profession."

"You should," Speller encouraged, then launched into memories of his life past. "I recall as a youngster; I had the desire to know more about everything. In fact, growing up in an orphanage, the nuns called me Shakespeare; the other kids called me a bookworm. I read everything I saw that had printing on it, even the cereal boxes, the Sears catalog, or advertisements that the local people I ran errands for saved for me.

"People thought it was unusual for a kid my age to be so interested in reading whatever he could find. I guess I was about ten when the nuns allowed me to help the seniors that were members of the church connected with the orphanage." I was a jack of all trades, helping with mowing, errands—whatever they needed." Speller grinned, remembering the kindness and encouragement he received from the nuns regarding his pursuit of knowledge.

"You were raised in an orphanage?" Friday looked surprised. "When I read your background, it said you were the son of missionaries and that you were born and raised in China."

"Don't believe everything you read. It's true that I lived with missionaries in China. In fact, I spent most of my life in China and the surrounding countries, but I was born and lived in an orphanage in a small town called Georgetown in Ohio. Have you ever heard of it?"

"Heard of it? This is uncanny. That's where I was born and where my grandparents lived. It's where I spent my summers as a kid," Friday replied.

"Well, I'll be darned. It's a small world, as the saying goes." They both sipped their tea as they contemplated this. Speller was anxious to learn more about the young man he had hired to work with him.

"I hope I'm not getting too personal, but I would like to get to know more about you," Speller said in an apologetic tone.

"Not much to tell. I was born in Georgetown, Ohio, and I was an only child. My mother was nineteen when I was born, and I never knew my father. My mom assumed that he had joined the navy after he left Ohio. She received a small bronze statue of Quan Yin he sent to her from China. She never heard from him again. There was no information about him when she began making inquiries with the army and navy for his records, so she assumed he was dead."

Speller sat mesmerized as Friday told of his background. The confirmation he had been searching for was unfolding. Astonishment paled on his face.

"And what did your mother do then?" he asked, his voice cracking with emotion.

She and I lived with her parents. She finished college and is still a practicing attorney. She married my stepdad when I was five years old, and we moved to Cincinnati, where she still lives.

"My stepdad was shot while on duty some twenty years ago. Mom never remarried. We stay in touch by telephone." He took a long sip of his tea.

"My mom is most interested about the work I'm doing as Friday and wants to learn more. The last time we talked, she told me that she would be here in Houston at the end of next month on business. Perhaps I can introduce you. She's reading several of your books that I recommended."

Speller sat and listened attentively, exuding obvious compassion that overwhelmed him with memories from the past.

He took a deep breath, punctuated by several uneven gasps, before he asked, "What was your mother's maiden name?"

"She was Christina Barlow until she married my stepdad. Now she is Christina Sander. She still goes by that name. Her friends call her Chris. I really would appreciate it if you could meet her while she's here. She would be thrilled,"

The shock of discovery from the information Speller was hearing hit him full force. He sat for a moment, his mind blank, very shaken.

Friday had opened up to this man and suddenly felt a kinship with him that he had never felt with anyone since his stepdad died. Perhaps it was the jasmine tea?

"Now, I have a question for you," Friday said. "For the past two months, the statue of Quan Yin has come to my attention three times. Olivia's statue in her yard. She explained how it came about being there. My mother's that was sent to her by my dad, and the one on your patio. Does yours have an interesting background or a meaningful story?"

Speller was silent. For some time now, he had been suspecting what had just been confirmed for him.

The intercom on Speller's desk buzzed, bringing him back to reality.

"It must be important. I'd better get it," Speller said as he got up to answer it. "I told Beth we were not to be disturbed."

He spoke quickly to Beth, then turned to Friday, holding out the phone. "It's for you. Someone named Ann is trying to locate you."

Friday's expression was serious as he spoke to the person on the other end. "I'll catch the next plane out. I'll go directly to the hospital. I'm so glad you were able to contact me."

He hung up and turned to Speller. "That was my mom's best friend. Mom was in a car accident, and it's serious. She's in the operating room as we speak."

"I'll go with you," Speller said.

"That won't be necessary."

"Nonsense, I want to. No need stopping to get anything. We can go directly to the airport. I'll have Beth check on flights to Cincinnati, and she can call my cell phone. I'll just need to get a draft that I'm working on. You may be able to help me," he said as he picked up a folder from his desk. Friday was stunned at the news he had just learned from Ann and appreciated Speller's support.

When they reached the airport, Speller already had the airline, flight number, and gate where they would board the plane.

Once they were settled in their seats, Speller told Friday that he needed his input on a story he recently started. "It will keep our minds occupied until we get there," he explained.

Speller steered the conversation to the book that he was currently writing entitled *First Love Reunited.* "I would like your honest ideas, questions, and opinions about the story," he said.

"I don't know how much help I can offer, but under the circumstances, I will do my best," Friday said.

"Before you begin reading, I'd better explain my method of writing. I write a skeleton. There is no dialogue, character descriptions, or scene development. It's an essay that needs a lot of padding so that the reader can identify with the characters and the surroundings. Many readers are familiar with the location where the story takes place, so you have to do research if you are not familiar with the setting.

"A good story needs humor, action, suspense, and drama. It can be both entertaining and informative. All my stories are 'faction'—fact plus fiction.

"After you finish reading my skeleton, I have a few questions. It helps me determine where to elaborate with more details. Do you get the picture?"

Speller had given Friday a crash course on his approach to writing his stories. Opening up his file folder, he pulled out a copy and handed it to Friday. He watched as Friday began reading.

☐☐☐☐☐

The year was 1987. The place was a small town called Marble Falls, Michigan, where Thomas Braden met his first love. Her name was Christina Chandler, the only child of a wealthy family.

Her father was a judge and a well-respected man. Her mother was very protective of her daughter, wanting the best for her.

When they became aware that their daughter was smitten with a 'nobody,' they forbade her to see him.

Christina was a headstrong girl and disobeyed their wishes. Thomas and Christina would meet secretly. First love can be so dramatic, especially when you are restricted and seventeen.

Their secret meetings were discovered, and her parents decided that it was in Christina's best interest to send her to spend the rest of the summer with an aunt who lived in another state.

The love affair between Christina and Thomas resulted in Christina becoming pregnant and bearing a son.

MAIN CHARACTER: Thomas Braden was raised in a Catholic orphanage. At the age of one, his parents were killed instantly in a car crash. He survived the crash. Everyone thought it was a miracle. He was thrown clear but suffered severe burns on his legs. The car exploded, and there was no identification to inform their next of kin.

To no avail, local authorities continued to try to locate information about the child's parents. Thomas Braden, the name they gave the boy, was made a ward of the state.

Because of his badly burned legs, no one that provided foster care wanted the responsibility of taking care of him. That's when Sister Agnes, Mother Superior of the Catholic orphanage, took him in.

The six nuns at the orphanage had fifty-four children ranging in age from infancy to seventeen. Because Thomas needed special attention and had difficulty walking, they spent more time with him.

At the age of three, he was able to read. At age six, he was reading to the other children. Eventually, he began walking without any aid after numerous skin grafts and surgeries.

One of Thomas's desires was to travel and to see the world. The summer he graduated from high school, he became a volunteer with the Junior Job Team. It was a church program that donated the boys' time doing odd jobs for seniors in the parish.

Also, the boys were hired to do painting and yard work for the people in the community.

Thomas was very frugal and saved every penny he earned that summer. The day that his new life began, he had $836.29 and memories that he would cherish, but they would also haunt him for the rest of his life.

He was eligible to continue his education on a scholarship program at the local college, but he had other plans. He had applied for a job on a freight ship that would be leaving for China in September. He was waiting to hear if he would get the job. If not, he would start college and wait for another opportunity.

He got the job.

He had no idea where Christina was. He wrote to her daily during his voyage and mailed the letters to her from every port where he had a layover. She had no way to contact him because he had no address, but she was constantly on his mind.

The Saratoga Freighter was definitely not a luxury liner. The crewmembers were bullies; the captain began drinking as soon as they left port, and Thomas stayed out of his way as much as possible.

The freighter made several stops during the month-long voyage. Thomas could have left the ship, but he had signed a contract, and China was where he was determined to go.

Before leaving, Thomas did a lot of reading and research about China. One of the stories he read was about Ruth Gamberg, who wrote about her experiences as a teacher in the mid-1970s in China.

"The wretchedness of the past is dead, and the Chinese are fashioning a new society to be inhabited by a new breed of human beings. Some Americans admired the Chinese Communists, particularly in the 1960s when they seemed to be achieving through communes and shared poverty, what U.S. radicals were preaching."

Thomas had no intention of following any political group; he just wanted to study and observe the culture. The only way he could achieve this, not knowing anyone or having any contacts, was to find one of the missionaries and start there. Since he was raised by nuns, this was the world he knew and with which he was comfortable.

St. Andrew's mission, located in the harbor district of China, was where he found his new home. The missionaries who were sent from England to save and convert the people were dedicated to their work and welcomed Thomas.

They recognized his ability as a fast learner, and in no time, he mastered the language. After two years, he was on the staff as a teacher. He learned to love the people and their dedication to service.

When he first arrived in China, he continued writing to Christina; he now had an address where he could receive mail.

When he was at the orphanage in Michigan, he had a close friend, Adam. He wrote Adam in hopes that he would give Christina a message from him. He sent the letter to the orphanage, assuming that Adam still lived there. The letter was returned with no forwarding address.

After a year with no contact from Christina, he came to the conclusion that it was not his destiny to continue to contact her.

As a final attempt to let her know that he still cared and loved her, he sent a small gift. He did not put a return address on the package for fear that if her parents saw that it was from him, they would not give it to her.

At age twenty-two, Thomas married a Chinese girl. They worked side-by-side as teachers in the mission. They had no children. During a street riot, his wife was shot in the crossfire.

Thomas was devastated, and shortly after the tragedy, he accepted the opportunity to go to England as a translator with one of the trading companies.

He welcomed this new opportunity, and while in England, he enrolled in college and spent the next six years in school studying every subject offered.

He had a childlike curiosity about life.

He married again at thirty-two, but sadly it only lasted four years. He met people from all walks of life, but his close friends were American news correspondents and reporters.

With his ability to speak and write six languages, Thomas was sought after as a consultant for a number of embassies in England. He was a world traveler, too restless to stay in any one place for too long.

When he was offered a position at a university in the United States, he accepted. He taught during the day and wrote his 'faction' in the evening. He deliberately did not pursue or investigate or try to locate

Christina. He assumed she had made a life for herself that did not include him.

But now, in his semi-retirement years, he felt compelled to find her, not to disrupt her life and family, but to have some sort of closure.

After Friday read the story, he sat in silence for several seconds, avoiding Speller's eyes. The manuscript pages were still clutched in his hand, the meaning of what he'd just read trying hard to edge its way into some sort of sense.

Finally, finding his voice, he asked softly, "How long have you known?"

Speller, too, found silence his friend. After a long pause, he drew in a deep breath. "That you're my son? Almost from the moment we met, Alex."

"Then why—why didn't you say something?"

"I had to be certain. When I asked your mother's maiden name, I knew the answer before you told me, but it was the confirmation I needed."

"Then this..." Friday lifted the manuscript from the small airplane table, "...this is your autobiography?"

"All writers include some of their personal experiences in their stories. I told you that it is 'faction.' There is still a lot of research still to be done." Speller gathered up his papers, put them back in his briefcase, and looked out of the window.

For a moment, Friday let his thought silently form in his mind, attempting to find the right words to say. "I recall something that fascinated me when I read your background and the titles of the books you authored. It said that you were a very complicated man and that few people were ever able to get too close to you. I find that to be true."

Friday laughed, paused for a moment, then continued, "The first day we met, I thought you would be formal and intimidating, but I got over it the more we talked."

"It pleases me to hear that. Now I have a confession," Speller said with a twinkle in his blue eyes. "The moment I saw you, I knew that you were the right man for the job, aside from the belief that you might be my son. I knew you were a person I could work with, and I think we have made a great team. I'm also confident that you have the talent to take the material you gathered thus far as Friday and make it into a best seller. It will be your story."

Friday stared at Speller, so surprised he was speechless.

"I have several other projects that I need to finish," Speller explained. "This latest story is my priority. I have the title and main character and a file full of anecdotes to make it a good read."

"Are you sure this story is not your autobiography?" Friday asked again.

Speller was silent as if searching for a plausible answer. On his face was a strange half-smile.

Expertly, he changed the subject. "I just happen to have two more letters requesting the services of Friday. One is from a twelve-year-old boy who wants to have a big brother for a month. It's quite touching. What do you think of that?"

He studied Friday's surprised but pleased reaction.

Their conversation was interrupted by the captain's announcement to fasten their seat belts in preparation for landing.

"We can catch a cab and go directly to the hospital," Speller said, turning to Friday, patting him on the shoulder. "She will be all right."

When they arrived at the hospital, Friday made inquiries at the front desk about his mother.

"She is out of surgery and in intensive care, down this hall and to your right," the nurse directed him.

When Speller and Friday entered the waiting room, Ann, his mother's best friend, was waiting.

"How is mother?" Friday asked.

"I spoke to the doctor briefly," she said. "He's concerned." She glanced at Speller, clearly wondering who he was and why he was there.

"I'm sorry, Ann," Friday said. "This is Sazz Speller, my boss. He insisted on coming with me."

"He's the author!" Turning to Friday, she said eagerly, "Your mother has been reading his books,"

After she introduced herself to Speller, she told Friday that his mother was in room three and that a nurse was with her. "She's in and out of consciousness and keeps calling for Thomas. I don't know who she is talking about. I never heard her mention a Thomas before."

When they walked into the room, the nurse was standing by the bed adjusting the IV. She glanced up and said, "You must be Thomas. She keeps asking for you." She directed the remark to Speller.

"I'm her son," Friday said, walking to his mother's bedside. He took her hand and whispered, "Mother, it's Alex."

There was no response.

He gently squeezed her hand, and suddenly, her eyelids opened. She focused on Speller, recognition hazy in her eyes; she said weakly, "Thomas, you came back. I knew you would. We have a son—Alex."

Speller walked to the other side of the bed and put his hand on her head, stroking her hair. In a voice filled with a mixture of compassion and sorrow, he said, "Yes, my beloved, I am here."

"I knew you would come. I knew you would come. I just knew." She sighed deeply, and the monitor beside her bed went flatline.

The nurse summoned help, and in what seemed like a split second, a doctor and two more nurses rushed into the room.

Friday, Speller and Ann were asked to leave. They went back into the waiting room where Friday paced back and forth, and Speller sat with his hands over his face sobbing softly.

After what seemed like an eternity, the doctor came from the room, his forehead lined in defeat.

"I'm sorry," he said to Friday. "We did all we could. We lost her. Had she lived, however, she would have been on life support the rest of her time."

He nodded to the nurse and walked away. She said with concern, "I need to have some papers signed so we can release the body to the morgue until you've made arrangements."

Friday followed her to the office to take care of the required details. When he returned, Ann suggested that she drive Speller and Friday to Christina's home. They followed her to her car, too exhausted to protest.

After they arrived at the house, Ann made coffee and informed Friday that several days prior, his mother had been discussing that when she died, she wanted to be cremated.

"At the time," Ann said, drying her tears, "I didn't think anything of it. Now I feel she knew that she wouldn't be here too much longer. She was in such good spirits today when we had lunch. I don't understand why she kept asking for Thomas."

She turned to leave with a promise that she would call them at 9:00 a.m. the next morning.

She turned to Speller and said, "Mr. Speller, it was so kind of you to come with Alex. Alex and his mother were so close, and now he has no family."

Speller looked at her and said, "My name is Thomas Braden. Sazz Speller is my pen name."

ADAM

"I'm ready to start my next assignment," Friday informed Beth. He had tossed and turned the night before.

It had been two weeks since his mother's death. Speller had stayed for the memorial service and supported Friday through his loss.

Speller's parting words when Friday took him to the airport were, "Stay as long as you wish. When you are ready to come back to Houston, we can sort things out if you wish to continue the research for the book."

"My immediate plans are to dispose of mother's personal belongings and to put her home on the market. There's nothing left for me here," Friday said. His sorrow was still a huge, painful knot inside.

Speller had left two letters that he had received requesting Friday's service. They had briefly discussed them on the plane on their way to Ohio. Now that the details of his mother's estate were completed, Friday was ready to leave.

As he gathered up the papers with transactions completed and pending regarding his mother's estate, he discovered the two letters that Speller had left.

The first was from a retired couple who wanted Friday to be their chauffeur to drive their travel camper cross-country to explore places of interest, which was something Friday had always dreamed of doing someday.

But it was the second request that got his attention, it was from a twelve-year-old boy who needed a big brother for a month while his mother went on a vacation to Europe.

The letter read:

Adam Sinclair
1512 Bossier Lane
Round Rock, OK 42311

Dear Friday:

My name is Adam, and I'm twelve years old. How would you like to be my big brother for a month while Mom goes on a trip she won? I don't want to stay with Mom's friend—she has two young children. She will, however,l be available if you need her, which isn't likely.

I play the fiddle, baseball, play chess, and Scrabble. I read a lot, too. I won't be any trouble, I promise.

My dad was killed in Beirut six months ago, and I miss him. Please say that you will come and stay with me. Mom checked you out. She helped me write this letter.

ADAM

After Friday read both letters, he made his decision—ADAM. That's when he called Beth and told her he was coming back to Texas and that he would contact the office when he arrived.

"I'm ready to play big brother to a twelve-year-old in Oklahoma," he told Speller when they met Monday afternoon.

The preliminary arrangements had all been made. It would only take a phone call to Adam's mother, Marie, to inform her that Friday was available and when would she like him to be there.

Friday talked to Marie personally while he was in Speller's office. She was elated when she heard Adam's letter was selected and that Friday would be his big brother. She told him about how Adam was expecting him and had made plans for his stay.

"He was so certain that you would be coming," she said.

It was agreed that Friday would be in Oklahoma on Thursday afternoon. Marie's flight was booked for Saturday. "That will give us time to get acquainted before I leave," she told Friday before they ended their conversation.

Everything was falling into place. Friday decided to drive his car, as he had plans to stay on and explore some of Oklahoma's points of interest. He was looking forward to the month ahead.

1512 Bossier Lane was a neat brick home in a development on the outskirts of Oklahoma City. It was shortly before 1:00 p.m. when Friday parked his car in front of the residence. As he opened the car door, a freckle-faced kid wearing blue jean shorts and a t-shirt that read MONTH OF FUNDAYS, ran out of the house to greet him.

Friday couldn't help but laugh. Who, he wondered, had thought of that?

"You must be Friday. Man, am I glad to see you. Mom is making peanut butter cookies. She's been cooking up a storm since yesterday—like we were going to starve." He grinned as he skipped ahead of Friday to the front door.

"He's here—he's here," Adam called out. The inviting, sweet aroma of cookies baking greeted Friday. Marie came out of the kitchen to meet him in the hallway.

Friday gasped ad blinked several times to make sure he wasn't seeing things like Olivia did. She resembled Trish, the woman he'd grown fond of during his stay in North Dakota when he was there to assist Olivia.

He recovered enough to stick out his hand and introduce himself. He noticed Marie wore her hair straight with bangs that covered her forehead; she wore no make-up and was quite attractive. Her hair was dark and glossy, her skin flawless, and her gray eyes were accented with shades of green that seemed luminous in the brightly-lit room.

As if sensing his approval, Marie immediately broke eye contact, lowering her head.

She turned to Adam and said, "Why don't you help Friday bring in his belongings and show him to his room? I'll make some iced tea, and we can solve the world's problems."

Friday flinched.

"That's supposed to be a joke," Adam explained on the way to the car, rolling his eyes. After they returned and took Friday's luggage to his room, they joined Marie in the kitchen.

Friday took a seat at the large table. Adam grabbed a cookie and said, "Now I want you to meet my best friend, Brutus."

As Friday looked around to see if he had overlooked someone, Adam opened the patio door and whistled. "A brindle Boxer ran in, and Adam snapped a leash onto his collar. "I'm training him to be our guard dog. We got him from the pound, and he was mistreated, so he needs a lot of love to forget his past," Adam explained in a serious tone.

The dog stood and sized up Friday, looking at Adam, then at Marie. They were both smiling and nodding their heads as if approving Friday.

Brutus finally relaxed, blowing air out of his nostrils as if to say, "If they approve of you, then so will I."

Adam let some slack out in the leash, and Brutus crossed the few feet of kitchen floor that separated them. He stood tight against Friday's leg and put his head on his knee.

Friday ruffled and stroked Brutus's coat, scratching him behind the ears while Adam watched. Brutus' nubby tail wagged in gratitude.

"See, I knew that Friday would like him," he said to his mother. "He's my responsibility," he emphasized, looking at Friday.

"Want to see my room?" he asked after taking a big gulp of tea.

"Sure," Friday replied. He got up and followed Adam down the hall.

The room was furnished with a desk with books and papers neatly stacked, a bookcase with a set of encyclopedias, a music stand, a violin, and a bulletin board overflowing with messages written on colored note squares. The number of notes got Friday's attention.

He stepped over to investigate when Adam explained, "Oh, those are my reminders to do chores. It's a woman thing, Dad used to say. She tacks up notes everywhere. It's just a reminder, Mom always says." Adam spoke in an easy, light-hearted manner.

"Each color represents a day. Green is Saturday and Sunday. Blue is Monday and Tuesday. Yellow is Wednesday and Thursday, and white stands for Friday. Mom teaches special education classes, and Dad used to tease her about bringing her work home with her."

Friday stepped closer to read the notes. The Monday green one said, "Change the bedding." Tuesday was trash day. Wednesday was at least an hour of fiddle playing or composing. Thursday—call or go see grandma. Friday, TV night until 11:00 p.m. Saturday, give Brutus a bath. Sunday—church and eat out.

"She tacks up a pink one once in a while to get my attention. Sometimes it's a joke, a compliment for something I did, or just a reminder that says, 'I love you.' Dad and I played her game, and he would leave messages for her around the house, too. Like I said, it's her thing. Did you notice the bulletin board in the kitchen? There are notes left for you—mostly phone numbers." His eyebrows raised as if he waited for Friday's reaction.

"I think that writing notes is a good way to remind and mostly to remember things," Friday said.

"Don't you think it's a little much?"

"No. My dad was a detective and carried a notebook with him at all times. He explained it was to get the facts straight. As a kid, I thought it was cool and carried a notepad with me, too. Some people list things in their daily journal, make grocery lists, or have an appointment calendar. In this busy society with so much going on, one sometimes tends to forget things."

Friday suddenly realized he was making excuses for his own note-taking habit, and he found it amusing that Marie also had the habit. Changing the subject, he focused on the violin. He noticed that Adam's name was inlaid on the chest of the instrument.

"Your letter said that you play the fiddle. When did you start playing?" Friday asked as he bent down to examine it closer.

"I was four years old when Grandma Wilma taught me. She built this one for me when I was ten. She also made a small one that I could handle better when my hands were smaller. She has it in her collection. I'll show it to you when we go to visit her next week. Do you play?" Adam asked.

"No, but I appreciate listening to any stringed instrument. I read someplace that the melody of a violin imparts a healing quality. Ever hear of that?"

"I don't know about healing, but I do know that I feel good when I play."

"I'm looking forward to hearing you play. Do you play in the orchestra at school?"

"Yes, but I like playing at bluegrass festivals best. You will still be here when we have our jamboree at the Shawnee County Fair."

They walked back into the kitchen just as Marie was drying her hands on a dishtowel.

"We're invited to my friend Kay's place this evening. Her husband, Frank, loves to cook out. They are looking forward to meeting you," she said as Friday sat back down to continue their conversation. "She lives close by if anything comes up that you may need help with. Adam is pretty dependable, but you never know," she added.

"That's good to know, but I have a feeling we will get along fine."

Friday was certainly not going to tell her that this was to be his first experience spending a month with a twelve-year-old. The only children that he had been around were the offspring of his co-workers at company picnics or office parties. He had always toyed with the idea that one day he would find the perfect mate, have children, and live happily ever after, as the saying goes.

The brief time he had spent with Adam, he was impressed with how mature the boy was. *It really is going to be a MONTH OF FUNDAYS, as Adam's t-shirt read,* he thought.

"I hope 'Weirdo' does a disappearing act and isn't there tonight," Adam said.

Marie looked at her son and said, "I thought we agreed that we wouldn't talk about him."

"But Friday needs to know what a jerk he is," Adam insisted. Marie hugged her arms over her chest as if trying to cut off unkind thoughts about her friend's stepson.

Oscar came to live with Kay and Frank when his mother could no longer handle him. After hearing and observing Oscar, she concluded that he was in need of counseling, but it certainly was not her place to interfere.

"He wants to be called STING," Adam emphasized. "His real name is Oscar. I can't blame him for wanting a different name, but STING? Makes you wonder how he came up with that—probably the rock star. You will notice," Adam wrinkled his nose in distaste, "if you look closely at his hair, he bleaches it."

"Adam! Enough of that!" Marie said, changing the subject. "Look at the time. It's almost four. Friday may need to rest, freshen up or unpack. We will leave the house at six o'clock." Turning to Adam, she said, "And young man, you can play with Brutus or take him for a walk."

☐☐☐☐☐

As Friday, Adam and Marie arrived at Kay and Frank's house; Adam noticed Marge's car parked in the driveway.

"Oh no, not her," Adam moaned. "Take Charge Marge is here, too. She's Frank's mother. She's just a hair net away from a fast food server."

Friday looked at Marie, who was attempting to keep a straight face. She just shook her head.

"He comes up with some off-the-wall observations. Don't encourage him. Guess he gets it from watching too much television."

"Right. I heard it on a sitcom a couple of nights ago, and I've been trying to think of someone who fits that description," Adam said, adding, "And she's it."

A scattering of toys served as lawn and walkway ornaments as the three walked toward the front door.

Before Marie knocked, a lanky teenager opened it. His forced grin was more of a smirk as he said to Adam, "I wouldn't have missed meeting your babysitter for all the fun my gang has planned for tonight."

"And this is Oscar, a rebel without a cause," Adam grinned.

107

"The name is STING!" Oscar corrected him as Marie's friend Kim came to welcome them. Her two children, Kristen, age four, and Nancy, age two, were behind her.

Kay was a beauty. Tall, slim, and tanned, she had her sun-bleached hair in a ponytail and a beauty pageant smile that was genuine. "Frank is putting the chicken on now. He made his special hickory sauce from scratch."

It was obvious that she was proud of him.

"I see that you met Oscar," Kay said. "He is responsible for mowing the grass in the backyard. He did a fine job trimming the overhanging branches on the patio, too."

Friday could tell Oscar was pleased that she was complimenting him.

Frank put his cooking fork down when he saw everyone enter the yard. He wore a plaid apron and a wide, friendly smile.

"Hope you like chicken," he called out as he walked toward Friday to shake his hand.

Frank's mother, Marge, in her mid-sixties, got up spryly to greet everyone.

Friday struggled not to laugh as he recalled Adam's take on her.

Friday, and Frank hit it off immediately. Frank worked as an adjuster for a major insurance company. As they got acquainted, they found that they had many common interests. Both were avid sports fans, and both enjoyed classical music.

Frank shared some of the most interesting case histories in his work, and Friday related some of the experiences he had when he spent time with the Skylarks.

Frank and Friday sat on lawn chairs with TV trays; the rest of the group was seated around a patio table.

Suddenly Marge got up and joined them with a bowl of cole slaw. She began spooning a generous serving on Friday's plate. Her son watched and patiently said. "Mom, Friday may not like slaw."

"Nonsense—everyone likes slaw. Are you forgetting that my recipe won first place two years in a row at the county fair?"

Friday had already tasted the slaw and still had some on his plate. Looking up at her, he said, "I can see why you won. This is the best slaw I've ever eaten." And he meant every word.

With that note of encouragement, Marge put the bowl down and pulled over her chair to join them. "What do you think about Marie traipsing all over the world and leaving Adam with a total stranger? And so soon after, her husband was killed."

"Mother! That was over six months ago," Frank reminded her.

She ignored him and continued, "This modern generation just doesn't use common sense. I offered to stay with Adam, but he wanted a big brother. I can see why he didn't want to stay with Kay and Frank. Kay has her hands full with the girls and now Oscar, who insists on being called Sting. Oscar is a perfectly good name. That was my husband's name. Oscar was a good man. I took care of him for thirteen months before he lost his battle with cancer."

Friday listened politely, nodding his head as she continued.

"Do you know what the name Oscar means? I looked it up in one of those name books. It means thoughtful, dignified." She glanced over at Oscar who was sitting on the patio swing sipping a soda.

Frank finally got his say and, turning to his mother with a practiced smile, said, "I'm sure a big brother is what Adam needs at this time. He and his dad were very close, and he seems to really like Friday. I think it's a good arrangement."

The little girls were giggling as Adam made funny faces while telling them a story.

Oscar, who sat watching, suddenly called out to Adam, "You're such a nut."

"Walnut or peanut?"

"What?"

"If I'm a nut, I want to know the variety. Clue me in."

Oscar looked confused. He got up and walked toward the house.

Frank and Friday overheard what transpired. "I wish I knew what happened to those two. When Oscar came two months ago, they hit it off, and I felt relieved," Frank explained. "He was having trouble at school in Iowa, where he lived with my ex. She couldn't control him, so she sent him to live with us. He's fourteen and only one grade ahead of Adam. Now he's mixed up with a local gang." His tone was apologetic, and Friday could tell he was very concerned. "Before school let out for the summer, I had to meet with his teachers and principal. The principal asked if he had a hearing problem. One of the older teachers said that she thinks all teenagers have selective hearing, that it's a curse, and she's starting to notice it now, even in the younger kids. She said he needed counseling."

"Maybe that's not such a bad idea," Frank responded. "Sometimes an outsider can reach a child better than a parent."

"Kay and I are wondering what caused the rift between Oscar and Adam. They hit it off so well until about a month ago when Oscar changed. He won't talk about it except to say that Adam is a square. Perhaps you can get Adam to tell you what happened."

"I can't make any promises, but if it comes up, I'll get back to you."

☐☐☐☐☐

The next morning Friday awoke to the smell of coffee. After a quick shower, he joined Marie in the kitchen. She was reading the paper.

"Adam is off to Little League practice," she said. "This will give us time to go over some last-minute details and our routine. We can take a tour of the town when Adam gets back."

"Sounds like a good idea," Friday said.

"How does a bagel with cream cheese and oatmeal sound? That is what Adam suggested for you." She laughed. "Seriously, what do you usually eat?"

"Bagel and oatmeal sounds great. It's been some time since I sat down to a bowl of oatmeal."

They were still lingering over coffee when Adam burst in the back door with his two friends, Chris and Josh. They came directly from ball practice.

"They wanted to meet you Friday. They think that having a big brother is neat. We play the Cougars tomorrow night. Chris is the pitcher, Josh is left field, and I'm the catcher. Mom will be gone, and you can meet the rest of the team after the game," Adam informed Friday in one big breath.

The two boys just stood looking at Friday with their mouths hanging open. Friday used his natural ability to make people feel comfortable and began asking them questions about the game. The conversation would have continued, but Marie reminded Adam that they had a lot of things to cover before she left.

☐☐☐☐☐

Friday found the tour around Round Rock had all the conveniences and still retained its small-town charm and personality. Oklahoma City was only fourteen miles away. The majority of the population was Native American. They still sold their crafts in the gift shops around the square.

"We even have a movie theatre," Adam pointed out as they passed a modern building with a black marble front on the square.

They stopped for lunch at Sam's. "This is the best place in town to get a burger. They make curly fries," Adam said as they walked through the door.

As Adam finished the last curly fry soaked with ketchup, the owner came over to introduce himself. Before he could say anything, Adam blurted out, "This is Mr. Sam, our team sponsor. He never misses a game."

"So you're the big brother we've been hearing about?" He smiled as he shook Friday's hand. "This calls for a celebration." He turned to the counter where a waitress stood and said, "Cindy, bring this table a raspberry sundae on the house."

"Neat!" Adam grinned and reached across the table.

Friday responded without hesitation.

111

They slapped palms in a modified high-five. Marie watched. A look of satisfaction lit up her face, and she felt content that she was doing the right thing by having Friday, a total stranger, come into their lives to look after her son. They were bonding.

That evening, while Marie was in her room packing and taking care of last-minute phone calls, Friday and Adam played Scrabble. Friday felt like a kid again as they sparred. They had just finished their second game when Marie walked into the room.

"Who's winning?"

Adam cracked a smile and replied, "I would have let him win out of courtesy and respect for his age, but before I had a chance, he won by cheating."

Marie looked at Friday and grinned.

"Good thing we weren't playing Russian roulette," Adam added. "My brains would be all over the kitchen."

"I don't cheat. I just employ advanced and complex techniques."

It was amazing how well the three of them hit it off. Marie was almost tempted to cancel her trip and stay home to enjoy Friday's company.

"I hate to be a spoilsport, but it's getting late, and we have an early start to the airport in the morning. Better call it a night and continue your sparring some other time."

"Just one more game?" Adam pleaded.

"Your mother is right. Let's call it a day—we've got a whole month together," Friday agreed as he got up.

"I'll knock on your door at 6:00 a.m., and we can have coffee," Marie said. "There is a breakfast bar at the airport that makes a fantastic omelet. Adam and I have eaten there on several occasions when we took Rob to catch a flight. He did a lot of traveling."

"Oh, Friday, you'll like their Spanish omelet topped with hot sauce. Good idea, Mom," Adam added.

It was 7:00 a.m. when they left for the airport. Friday drove his car. Marie asked questions about his last assignment, and Adam chimed in wanting to hear more details about his experiences as they drove to the airport.

The breakfast bar was not too crowded. They found a table in the back that gave them more privacy.

"I'd love to hear what a gabfest between the two of you is like when I'm not here to provide some rationality," Marie said.

"You provide rationality?" Adam asked playfully. "Bet if Dad were here, he would agree. He would say that you were biased with all your wisdom and rationality. The rest of us have to rely on our knowledge." Turning to Friday, he asked, "Do you know the difference between wisdom and knowledge?"

"I've never given it any thought," Friday replied.

"Knowledge is book learning. Wisdom is the ability to use knowledge to make common sense judgments. That's the way Dad explained it."

"That makes a lot of sense. Your dad must have been a great guy. I wish I'd had the opportunity to meet him."

After breakfast and saying their goodbyes, they made their way to the security line. Marie promised to call the minute she was in the hotel in Portugal, her first stop on the tour.

"And by the way…"

"Yes, I know," Adam said. "It's Saturday, and Brutus gets a bath."

"That's my boy," she said as she gave him one last hug before she went through the security gate.

The trip back home was uneventful.

"That last jelly donut requests peace and quiet so it can digest," Adam said as he wiggled himself into a position for greater comfort.

Friday was busy with his own private thoughts. He wanted to get a report off to Speller. He would email a brief update and write out a detailed description of the people he had met since arriving. He was certain that Speller would enjoy Adam's take on Marge—'a hairnet away from a fast food server.'

That afternoon when Friday went out to sit on the patio with a book and a glass of iced tea, Brutus looked clean and comfortable.

Adam was damp, sweaty, and stank of dog shampoo. He was just gathering up the brush and shampoo and was eager to get his shower and change. He had worked up an appetite.

Friday said that he would fix their lunch. "Does pasta salad and muffins sound okay? That's what Kay brought over last evening."

"Sure," Adam said. "She makes the best shrimp and pasta salad I ever tasted. Hope she fixed enough."

Friday took their plates out to the patio, and Adam joined him, fresh out of the shower and ready to dig in.

Brutus lay close, watching Friday and Adam eat. Suddenly an orange and black butterfly swooped past Brutus's face, startling him. He barked once and raced after it, off the patio, across the grass. Dashing back and forth across the lawn, leaping high, snapping at the air, he repeatedly missed his target.

Suddenly he collided with the trunk of a tree as Friday and Adam watched.

Adam looked over at Friday and said, with a giggle, "Brutus is not the sharpest knife in the drawer."

Friday grinned. He never ceased to be amazed at what this twelve-year-old going on fifty had to say.

☐☐☐☐☐

The Cougars lost by two points that evening as Friday watched the game. The coach assured them that they had played their best, but someone had to lose.

"Next time, guys, it's our turn to win."

Friday was impressed with what an easygoing guy he was and why Adam spoke so highly of him. Friday met the team and many of their parents. Kay, Frank, and the girls were also there.

"We never miss a game," Kay said.

Frank suggested that they meet at the ice cream parlor. Adam chatted about his teammates and entertained his two young friends while the adults got better acquainted.

On Sunday, Kay came by with the girls to take Adam to church. Friday stayed home and read the Sunday paper. The routine of daily living was flowing smoothly.

Over the next few days, with school out and the weather being unusually comfortable in June, Adam had his friends over. They batted the ball around the yard, climbed trees, played with Brutus, then played chess or watched television in the evening.

Wednesday, after dinner, Adam reminded Friday, tomorrow they would go to visit Gram Wilma and Gramp James. He began telling Friday about them.

"You will like Gram Wilma. She has wisdom. Gramp James is quite a talker, but man, is he a good fisherman. Once, he caught an eighteen-pound catfish. That was before he fell and hurt his knees, and got arthritis. Dad, Gramps, and I used to go fishing at the pond they have at the back of their property. Maybe you and I can go fishing while you're here."

Friday's face lit up. "I didn't bring my fishing gear, but I really enjoy the sport."

"No problem. I have a tackle box full of lures, and we have plenty of rods and reels. Dad used to fish with Gramps while Gram taught me to play the fiddle."

The next morning as Friday and Adam were heading to visit Gram and Gramps, Adam continued telling Friday about his family.

"Gram Wilma is not my mom's biological mother. Mom was raised in an orphanage. When she was fifteen, she had the opportunity to live with the Watsons, Gram, and Gramps."

The fifteen-mile trip in a rural area where his grandparents lived passed swiftly as Adam talked.

"They treated her like their daughter. She called them Mom and Dad. After college, she met Dad. He was a photographer with the paper in Oklahoma City. They moved here. I was born here and decided to stay so I could be near my parents." Adam paused and looked at Friday.

Friday shook his head, wondering if he heard right.

Adam grinned. "Just wondering if you were listening or bored."

"Bored, never. Listening and interested, yes."

"So I'll continue to fill you in on the life and times of my mom's family. Mom calls them every week or so. I think Dad considered them like his parents—you know."

Friday wanted to know more about this relationship. "In what way?"

"In what way—what?" Adam asked.

"You said that your Dad considered them like his parents."

"Yeah, well, he didn't have any family that he ever talked about. When I asked Mom if I had grandparents, she said that I was lucky to have Gram and Gramps. Guess it was their secret."

They finally arrived at their destination—a modest clapboard house that looked like it had not received any maintenance in a long time.

Silvered by years of insistent sun, bare wood showed through peeling paint like dark bones.

At the end of the gravel driveway, a battered Ford pickup stood on bald tires under a sagging carport.

Gram Wilma was waiting for them as they got out of the car. She had a smile on her face as Adam walked over to hug her.

"And this is Friday, my big brother," Adam said.

"I don't see any family resemblance," Gram grinned and winked at Friday. Friday guessed this was where Adam got his quick sense of humor.

They walked to the house, and Gram showed them inside.

The furniture in the living room seemed to be on the brink of spontaneous combustion. The sliding windows were open to admit a draft, but the June day declined the invitation to provide a breeze.

In the kitchen, the table was already set. A small electric fan sat on the kitchen floor, churning the warm air with less cooling effect than might be produced by a wooden spoon stirring the bubbling beans she was cooking on the stove.

"I made cornbread, pinto beans, and chow-chow for lunch. I hope you're hungry. I know Adam always is. Marie and Adam helped me make the chow-chow last fall when we had a bumper crop of green tomatoes." She looked at Adam and smiled.

Gram wore a shapeless housedress. She was in her mid-sixties. Her flyaway mouse brown-gray hair was as lusterless as dust bunnies.

Her face was enlivened by a wealth of freckles, and her voice was musical and warm. Friday liked her immediately.

From the far end of the house came a slow, rhythmic thumping. Adam's Gramp James was making his way toward the kitchen.

"I hope you don't mind it being so warm. James has arthritis and can't stand to be cold. I'm used to it," Wilma said as she poured tea into the ice-filled glasses on the table. Friday wiped the sweat from his brow with his hand when she wasn't looking.

James finally entered the kitchen, poling himself along on a pair of sturdy canes. He, too, was in his middle sixties, but he looked twenty years older.

Blame time for his thinning white hair, but his ruddy, bloated face was the consequence of illness and medication. Rheumatoid arthritis had twisted his hips. He should have graduated to crutches or a walker, but pride kept him on the canes.

Pride, too, had kept him on the job long after pain should have prevented him from working. Unemployed now for five years, he was trying to live on disability payments.

He swung into the chair and hooked the canes to the back of it. Wilma introduced Friday to her husband.

He held out his right hand to Friday. The hand was gnarled, the knuckles swollen and misshapen.

"You're a right fine-lookin' young man," he said by way of greeting.

Friday pressed it lightly, afraid of causing pain even with a gentle touch.

"Adam, are you ready for Saturday's jamboree?" Gramps asked, indicating for Friday and Adam to join him at the dining room table.

"I sure am, and so is Friday."

Turning to Friday, Gramps said, "Tell me about yourself." He looked into Friday's eyes with hawk-like intensity. "It takes a special person to volunteer to keep an eye on a boy for a month, and you not being related. We would have had him here, but when we heard that he won your services, we were relieved." He glanced at his wife and saw her frown at his remark. Changing the subject, he continued, "Have you heard Adam play the fiddle?"

"Yes, I have. He entertained me one evening by playing a CD as an accompaniment. I also hear him practicing. He certainly has talent."

Gram Wilma interrupted with the announcement that lunch was ready and brought steaming bowls to the table. Friday stood up to help her.

"Adam doesn't just have talent. He is gifted!" Gramps emphasized, picking up his knife and buttering his hot cornbread. "Wilma taught the boy, you know—when he was four years old. He picked it up like a pro." It was obvious that Gramps enjoyed his opportunity to share his opinions. "Did Adam tell you that the local fiddlers are entertaining this Saturday at the fairgrounds? They are getting fired up for the bluegrass festival that is held every fall in Oklahoma City."

"Yes, Gramps, I already told him that we are going. Gram and I will be playing *On Hallowed Ground*, the song she wrote when she was my age."

"That's always been one of my favorites," Gramps sighed as he nodded his head in approval. "So, Adam, what brings you out here today?"

"I want to show Friday Gram's collection of fiddles and her shop where she repairs them for the pickers. And I wanted Friday to experience Gram's delicious beans and cornbread."

"Did Adam tell you that Wilma is known all over the world for her knowledge and workmanship, for building and repairing fiddles?" Gramps asked.

Gram just sat quietly, watching everyone enjoy the meal she had prepared, and smiled at her two staunch admirers, James and Adam, as they praised her. Hames prattled on about the particulars of their life all throughout the meal.

After they finished eating, Wilma got up and cleared the table. When she was finished, she said to her husband, "Dishes can wait. They came to see my workshop," And before he could say anymore, she led them to the back door.

James had to make sure he had covered all bases about his talented spouse. "Adam, show Friday where she keeps all her awards."

"It's in her office, this way," Adam said as he led the way.

She has an ego room instead of an ego wall. Good for her, Friday thought.

After Friday admired and examined her trophies and plaques, they headed for her workshop in back of the house.

Not finished yet; James still had information to share with Friday. He was still sitting at the table while Adam showed Friday Wilma's awards.

"Hold up a minute; you got to hear this," he yelled before they went out the back door. "Four years ago, Wilma was in a movie that was shot in Oklahoma City. They had her playing the fiddle in their bar scenes. That Redford guy, you know, the actor, was a nice person. He let me stay on the lot and eat with the crew while she worked for him."

"James, I think Friday has heard enough about me. He came to see the shop," Wilma reminded him.

"No, I'm fascinated with all the talent and gifts Wilma and Adam have. I would be proud of them, too. Thank you for sharing."

Friday was impressed and genuinely interested as he listened to Wilma and Adam point out and explain the makings of a fiddle, including what it took to produce the best tone.

Wilma had even built a metal fiddle and played it for Friday to demonstrate the different tones.

They talked about twelve-time Grammy Award winner Ricky Skaggs. He came to her shop and had her repair one of his instruments.

Adam was only nine at the time, and Gram told Marie to bring Adam out so he could meet Ricky. "He was a nice enough guy," Adam said. "And, man, can he play."

Driving home that afternoon, Adam was still answering questions that Friday asked.

"So they can't use amps at bluegrass festivals?"

"Don't need to. Wait until you hear some of the old-timers belt out their music. It can shake the rafters."

After a long day, Friday was pleasantly tired. He thought he would fall asleep the moment he put his head on the pillow, but it didn't happen. He couldn't stop thinking about Trish and how much he wished she could be there with him.

It was Marie that had reminded him so much of Trish. She had the same color eyes and the same graceful, slender line of her throat, the musical sound of her laughter, the curve of her smile.

I'm in love. I miss the companionship of a partner, he admitted to himself. He would call Trish in the morning.

The house was quiet when Friday awoke. He looked at the bedside clock and assumed that Adam had already left for ball practice. When he entered the kitchen, Adam was at the table eating cereal and toast.

"You still here?" Friday asked.

"No, this is a clever cardboard façade. The real me is in the john shooting heroin."

Friday was once again caught off guard by Adam's response.

"Adam, do you memorize all the one-liners so that you can recite them on the spur of the moment?"

"I guess so. I just remember things I read or hear. Not many people have a sense of humor, and I enjoy getting a surprise response. Dad said I had a photographic and sharp mind and that I inherited it from his gene pool. Don't know if it's an asset or a liability. In some circles, it would be described as having a fresh mouth. I try to watch it when I'm around some people, like Gram and Gramps. No need to upset them, so I stay cool. If I come on too strong for you, I'll back off."

"No need for that. It's just that I had no idea a twelve-year-old could be so quick-witted."

"Friday, you really need to loosen up. When we first met, I got the impression that you were melancholy, almost sad. I figured that you were working through some unpleasant experience. Mom and I talked about it the first morning after you got here. She told me to back off and that you might be sensitive. 'No, he's just sad,' I told her."

"You were right. Just before I came here, my mother died in a car accident, and I still think about her and miss her," Friday explained.

"Me, too. I still miss my dad so much. I talk with him, you know, pretending that he's still here and in the room with me. Does that sound weird?"

"No, not at all. I think it's normal missing a person. Sometimes I even get the feeling that they are around us and can hear us."

"Promise not to laugh, and I'll tell you something." Adam became very serious.

"No, I won't laugh. I promise," Friday said.

"When Kay heard the contest on the radio about getting a man to spend a month helping someone out, she told Mom that I should write you a letter asking you to come and be my big brother. At first, I thought NO WAY! Then I asked Dad about it that night, and he was all for the idea. When I told Mom, she said, 'Let's go for it,' and now you are here, and you can be my big brother or my second dad forever."

"That sounds like quite a responsibility—forever. But I must confess, I wouldn't mind having you as my son."

"Friday, we are solving the world's problems. That's the way Mom explains it when we have our family discussions, especially when Dad was here."

"And by the way, I didn't go to ball practice this morning because I won't be playing. We are going to the fair. Remember, I'm playing my fiddle with Gram tonight. Let's leave early enough so we can walk around the fairgrounds."

☐☐☐☐☐

The day turned out to be a pleasant experience. Adam decided to leave his fiddle in the trunk of the car until it was time to warm up.

As they entered the grounds, there were rows and rows of tables with merchandise displayed.

Friday stopped, looking at the crowds—people eating ice cream in big waffle-cookie cones, people eating caramel apples on sticks wrapped in waxed paper.

There were guys in feather-decorated cowboy hats they'd bought from one of the vendors; groups of pretty young girls in short shorts and halters; a very fat woman in a purple muumuu; people speaking English and Spanish and Japanese and Vietnamese and all the other languages you might hear at any state fair.

Wow! What a colorful gathering of people," Friday thought.

Adam noticed a Slurpee stand. "Man, I haven't had a Slurpee in a long time. Do you want one?"

"Why not?" Friday replied.

They found a bench and sat down with their drinks, watching the passersby.

Suddenly, Adam turned to Friday and announced, "The next sound you hear is me enjoying the last half inch of my Slurpee."

Friday just shook his head, something that had become a habit with him since being around Adam.

"Ever thought of being a stand-up comic?" Friday asked.

"Nah, just like to see if I can get a rise out of you. You're loosening up more. Maybe the shirt that I've been wearing is helping. A MONTH OF FUNDAYS is my intent, and so far, it's working."

They continued to walk the grounds, stopping several times when they found something interesting, like a chubby girl drawing portraits of people with colored pastels. She was good.

Or one vendor sticking on pictures that looked like tattoos on people's legs and arms.

They finally found the area where the entertainment would be held.

The fiddle players were already congregating under the open-sided tent. The metal chairs were filling up with people waiting for the music to start.

Most of the players wore Stetsons or straw hats. Adam had on a western plaid shirt with studs instead of buttons, and he exchanged his shorts for blue jeans when he joined Friday after changing and getting his fiddle out of the car.

"I don't like to wear a cowboy hat," he said, adding. "Too hot."

The music finally began, and the audience clapped, whistled, and stomped their feet to the music.

The players that were to perform sat on the side of the platform, waiting their turn to be introduced. There were ensembles of four, three, duets and several solos.

Wilma appeared dressed in a blue jean skirt and a red and white ruffled western shirt and took a seat beside Adam in the performer's area. Friday looked around for James, but he didn't see him.

Adam and Wilma were the last to perform. When they were introduced, they received loud applause and piercing whistle approval. It was obvious they were the audience's favorite.

Friday experienced such a proud feeling that he got a lump in his throat. *o this was how parents felt when they watched their children perform.*

When Wilma and Adam left the platform, they walked over to join Friday. Friday gave Adam a hug and said, "Good job, buddy."

An elderly couple walked up to Friday. The man said, "You must be rightly proud of your son. I look for him to out-fiddle Ricky Scaggs one day."

Friday was at a loss for words and just looked at the man until Adam said, "He's my second dad for a month."

The man looked at the two and smiled. His wife, overhearing what transpired, turned to her husband and asked, "What was that all about?"

"Don't rightly know. Could mean anything."

When Friday inquired where James was, Wilma told him that James had fallen and sprained his wrist and wasn't able to join them. "He and the neighbor man were playing Canasta when I left," she explained.

◻◻◻◻◻

Little League played their last game of the season and won.

Friday and Adam went fishing and visited Wilma and James.

The movies, pizza feasts, visits with Frank and Kay, and chess sparring kept them busy. Marie called faithfully every night before Adam went to bed. He missed her a lot but was busy enough that he didn't express it openly.

Time seemed to fly. Friday was able to finish reading Speller's book.

It was Thursday of the third week that Friday had spent with Adam when Kay and Frank came by, visibly upset. They were concerned about Oscar. He had not been home for two days. Frank explained that he assumed Oscar went back to Iowa to be with his mother, but when they finally called her, she informed them she hadn't seen or heard from him.

Frank asked Adam if he knew where Oscar might be.

"No," Adam replied, "I haven't talked to him in some time. He may have gone camping with the guys he hung out with," was all he could tell them.

Kay had called several of Oscar's friends' parents, but no one had seen him.

Friday offered to help in any way he could.

After Kay and Frank left, Friday took the opportunity to ask Adam what went wrong with his friendship with Oscar. "You can see how upset Kay and Frank are; if you know anything, I feel you should tell them or me," he reasoned with Adam.

Adam sat silent, looking down at the floor. Suddenly he got up, went to his room, and returned with his tape recorder. "It's all on tape, and I don't know what to do with it," he said. "If only Dad were here, he would know what to do."

Friday saw a different Adam, a boy who was genuinely frightened.

"Tell me about it," he encouraged. "We can play detective and solve it together."

Adam finally began the tale. He told Friday about the gang of five boys who called themselves The Moles. They were always in trouble, taking lunch money away from kids at school, tripping kids in the hall, selling drugs.

"I stayed as far away from them as I could," he said. "When Oscar started school here, they called him an outsider, and he had a fight with one of The Moles. But a week later, I noticed that he was hanging out with them.

"One Saturday, he was over here while Mom and Kay went shopping. I had just finished bathing Brutus and had gone into my room to change clothes. He followed me and began bragging how he had conned The Moles and that he was now a member of the elite five. 'They plan on recruiting more members, and I told the Judge—he's the leader—that you might be interested.' He thought he was doing me a big favor."

Adam sighed and continued, "At first, I thought it was a joke because when we talked about the gang earlier, he referred to them as amateurs. But he sounded dead serious."

Adam continued to share all the details as Friday sat spellbound. About how he thought about getting the conversation on tape, perhaps playing it back for Oscar. Adam still thought it was a joke and that Oscar was a good actor.

The recorder was on his desk, as he often used it to record when he played his fiddle. He had turned it on without Oscar's knowledge and began asking questions.

Oscar began boasting what the initiation entailed—steal one hundred dollars, go to bed with a girl, have a tattoo with an 'M' on your left shoulder, meaning Mole, and you would have to sell drugs to the kids at school.

"They are a bunch of sickos," Adam said. "After Oscar left and I listened to the tape, I still thought it was a joke 'cause we had fun playing pranks on each other. I kept thinking it was a joke until the day Oscar showed me his tattoo. 'I'm in. I passed the initiation,' he'd bragged. 'Now I can recruit you as my second. We can have a blast.' I got scared and told him that I would think about it. A few days later, one of the guys who's a member—he calls himself The Terminator—came up to me real friendly and said that Sting had recruited me, and I was invited to go to a meeting the following night."

"He told me that they had big plans for one of the store managers in town who kicked a Mole out of his store for shoplifting."

As Adam continued to tell the story to Friday, the phone rang. It was such an unexpected intrusion that Friday almost fell out of his chair.

Adam answered it. Frank wanted to talk to Friday.

"Oscar is in jail in the next county. I just got a phone call from the police, and I'm going to pick him up. Thought you might like to know," Frank told him. Friday thanked him and offered his help should Frank need it. Then they hung up.

ADAM

Friday had been hanging onto every word Adam said and wanted to hear more. It sounded like the script for a Mafia movie with kids in their early teens playing the roles of seasoned crooks.

"So I got an idea how I could handle the situation," Adam continued after Friday finished his phone conversation. "I made three copies of the original tape. I have one hidden in my tackle box, one in the pocket of a shirt, and one on top of the dresser. The lead-in on each tape states that this tape should be turned over to the police. That's not original. I actually saw it in a movie and remembered that it worked."

"Then Oscar came over, still proud and enthusiastic, thinking that he was able to recruit me, but instead, he got the surprise of his life. I played the tape for him. It was so explicit with Oscar's bragging details that he just sat there red-faced and then got angry. He got up and pulled the tape out of the recorder and said, 'There goes your proof—so who will believe you?'"

Adam told him that he'd made three more copies and that the one Oscar had in his hand, he could play for his gang to hear, and if they laid so much as a hand on him, his dog, or his mother, he would give a copy to the police.

Oscar turned white and yelled out obscenities promising Adam that he wouldn't get away with it.

"But I have," Adam said. "I had to be cool and threaten them to leave me alone. I don't know how much Oscar told the gang, and I don't care. I just wanted them to leave me alone."

"Did you tell any of this to your mother?" Friday asked.

"Not yet. At first, she wondered why Oscar and I weren't friends anymore, and I told her he made new friends his own age. I didn't know what else to say. With Dad gone, I was the man of the house, and that means being strong and able to control things. Mom didn't nag me about it, and some things are best left unsaid. I think Oscar is afraid of me, and that's the way I like it."

"That's a lot of responsibility for any boy. I had no idea that high school kids were playing out the role of thieves, bullies, and thugs to this extent. Something should be done about this," Friday declared.

"Like what?" Adam asked.

"I'll listen to the tape tonight, and we can talk about it tomorrow. I'd also like to learn what Frank found out about Oscar's arrest."

There was little sleep for Friday that night after listening to the tape. All he could think about was Adam keeping that information to himself. Things like that had never happened to Friday when he was growing up—or maybe he was simply not aware of it.

The next morning while Friday was putting a bagel in the toaster, Adam walked into the kitchen. He was unusually quiet. Friday decided he'd better not bring up the subject of Oscar then. Adam got the Rice Krispies out of the cabinet, poured some into a bowl, added milk, and sat, playing with his food.

"Not feeling well this morning?" Friday asked.

"I miss Mom. She hasn't called in three days."

"I'll bet she's saving up all the extra exciting adventures to share with you when she gets home. She'll be back in less than a week," Friday said cheerfully.

That didn't seem to improve Adam's outlook. He went to his room and tried to get interested in a video game. It became quiet, and Friday assumed that the boy went back to bed or decided to read.

Friday took that opportunity, as he often did when Adam was otherwise occupied, to type out his notes to Speller. He really was beginning to enjoy writing. It made him more aware of people's personalities, something he never paid attention to before he began this assignment. Perhaps that was the reason Speller enjoyed writing.

It was after 1:00 p.m. when he knocked on Adam's door and called to him, "Can I come in?"

"The door is open," Adam replied.

"Let's go to Sam's for a burger and fries," Friday suggested. "I'm starved."

"You go. I want to stay home. Mom might call."

"Can I bring you back something?"

"Maybe a burger for later."

When Friday returned, Kay's car was parked in the drive. She was just getting out. They met on the walk.

"I came over to see about Adam," she said. "He sounded so down and out when I called. He said you were out getting burgers. My women's intuition kicked in, and I sensed that he was really missing Marie. So here I am."

They entered the house. Adam was still in his room. The door was ajar. Kay went to look and found Adam asleep.

"Let's let him sleep," she said. "The poor kid has been through so much, and he's usually so upbeat. I figure he misses Marie. They have such a good relationship."

As they sat in the living room, Kay told Friday about the trouble Oscar was in. He was caught over in the next county with five other boys robbing a convenience store at two in the morning. The boys had been drinking, and there was a teenage girl involved.

"It's quite a mess," Kay said. "Frank hired an attorney, and we'll have to wait to see how things turn out. In the meantime, Oscar is being held in juvenile detention."

"Have you heard from Marie?" Friday asked.

"Why, yes, we talked two days ago. She met an Italian who is an antique dealer. He travels back and forth from Milan to New York. She was in really good spirits. She thinks she's in love, says he's such a great guy. She was a bit concerned about how Adam would handle it. She said she would wait until she got back to tell him. It sounded serious."

That evening, Adam didn't want to come out of his room. He ate half of the burger he had zapped in the microwave.

Friday was able to cajole him into sitting and watching television with him before they retired for the night.

When Friday finally went to bed, he lay on his back, eyes open, wide awake. Pale amber light from the vapor lamp in the yard found its way through the shuttered windows. He tried to turn his mind away from thoughts of Adam's situation, but he found himself relentlessly tormented by thoughts of how he should handle it.

He desperately wanted to help see Adam through what he felt was a major crisis.

Sleep finally overtook him. Little did Friday realize what major challenges and decisions he would soon face—decisions that would change his life and the lives of everyone he had met in Round Rock, Oklahoma.

A New Beginning

It was 4:00 a.m. on Thursday when Adam burst into Friday's room. He was sobbing. "Mom—she's dead. He pushed her into the water. She drowned."

Friday bolted up in his bed, momentarily disoriented, awakened so suddenly from a sound sleep.

"Whoa, Whoa—hold on there. Where did you get that notion?" He rubbed the sleep out of his eyes and then lay back on one elbow.

"I saw it. The man with the scar on his hand pushed her off the boat. She drowned," Adam repeated.

"You just had a bad dream. We all have them now and then. He patted the bed, and Adam sat down. "They can be so real that we actually think that something is happening." Friday did his best to calm Adam.

Adam finally stopped crying and asked, "Then why doesn't she call?"

"She will. She is probably so busy that she forgot. We do that sometimes. I've done it. And I talked to Kay yesterday. She said that your mother is having a good time but is missing you. She's looking forward to showing us all the pictures that she is taking."

Adam only half listened.

What Friday didn't tell Adam was that Marie had met a man in Rome and that he had joined her on the tour. Marie had told Kay, "Don't tell Adam. I'll tell him when I get home."

"But it was so real," Adam insisted. "I never had this kind of scary dream before." Still visibly distraught, he shook his head back and forth, trying to force the image from his mind.

Friday tried to reason with him. "Your mother is not on a boat. Remember, we checked yesterday. The itinerary on the bulletin board lists that her group is now in Switzerland. Their last stop will be Germany. From there, they catch a plane to New York; then it's home to Oklahoma City."

Adam remained unconvinced, continuing to shake his head.

"I'll tell you what. Let's look at her itinerary again. I may be mistaken. There's nothing about a boat trip that I recall." Friday got out of bed, and they both went into the kitchen to check.

"Yep, here it is. She's still in Switzerland at the Zurich Hilton Hotel. Tomorrow they leave for Munich. They'll be staying at the Bayerische Hotel in Germany. I'll call in the morning. I don't know what time they'll be leaving, but I'm sure that we can track her down."

"When Mom and I talked last, she told me the time where she's at is about seven hours ahead of ours. Can we please call her now?"

Friday realized there would be no sleeping for either of them until Adam made contact.

"Good idea. I'll make the call, and we can put an end to your concern." Friday picked up the phone.

He had no problem getting through to the hotel in Zurich. He asked if the Browning Tour party was still registered.

"Yes, they are," the desk clerk informed him.

"Ring Marie Sinclair's room, please," Friday requested.

After a brief pause, the operator came back on the line, "Madam Marie Sinclair does not answer. Do you wish to leave a message?"

"Yes. Please inform her that she needs to call home as soon as possible."

Hanging up the phone, Friday looked at Adam and said, "It's done. That's all we can do tonight. It's about 11:00 a.m.; she's probably o a tour. She'll call."

Wide-awake now, Friday suggested they make some hot chocolate and toast. "We can play Scrabble while we wait for your mother to call."

Adam liked the idea and made the toast.

Friday began telling Adam about the time he was in Switzerland and how good their hot chocolate was.

"They even have a Starbucks and had an excellent drink with coffee and chocolate. It's called Mocha."

"Dad took Mom and me to a Starbucks in Tulsa once when we went on vacation. Can't remember what Dad ordered for me, but I remember it was good."

They talked and played Scrabble until the sun came up. Adam showed no sign of being sleepy. Friday could hardly keep his eyes open.

Abruptly he got up. "I know who we can call, the tour director. Her name is on the itinerary. She will know something. Maybe your mother took a side trip without the group."

Friday located the phone number and dialed. "We got lucky. She's in her room, and the operator is connecting us now," Friday told Adam who was standing beside him.

"Hello?" Amanda Browning answered.

Friday introduced himself as a friend of Marie's who has been watching her son.

"She hasn't called home in three days. She usually calls every day, and we are concerned," he informed her.

"I haven't talked to Marie in several days. She met a man in Rome, and he has been showing up at all our stops. I just asked her roommate, Gayle, where Marie is because we leave for Munich in two hours. I have a policy with people on my tours that they let me know if they change plans and wish to stay behind and catch up later, but she never told me anything. Her passport is still in the hotel safe, so I know that she didn't leave Switzerland.

"According to her roommate, Marie told her that she would be back in time to join the group for our trip to Munich." Her voice sounded edgy and tired as she sighed in exasperation. "I'm sorry I sound abrupt, but this trip has been no picnic keeping up with all these people who have different ideas as to where they want to go."

Friday was now determined to do what he could to solve this mystery. He called Kay to find out if she knew more about the man Marie was seeing.

"All she told me was that his name was Tony something. I do remember his last name started with an S—Strum...bouie—no, that doesn't sound right. I don't recall. We did joke, and I told her to be careful that rumor had it that the Italian men are great lovers. She was so upbeat I was happy for her. How is Adam handling all this?" she asked.

Friday told her about the dream Adam had and how he keeps insisting that she was pushed overboard from a boat.

"Oh, my God!" Kay cried. "I just remembered—Marie did tell me that a friend of Tony's had a party boat, and they were going to go on an evening cruise."

The blood drained from Friday's face. "I'll get back to you later, Kay, but I've got to make a phone call now—thanks for your help," he managed before he hung up.

He took a deep breath and called the police station in Zurich, explaining his concern about a friend who was missing. He informed the officer about the last person she was seen with, that his name was Tony. "I don't know his last name—it may start with an S—but my friend met him in Rome, and he had a scar on his hand."

"One moment, please," the officer said. "I want the chief to hear this."

When the chief got on the phone, Friday repeated all the information. "Yes, we are familiar with Tony Strumbona. He has a record sheet a foot long, and yes, we know about his scar. He is known to take advantage of wealthy tourists. Presently he has a drug trafficking charge against him. His address is Rome, but he shows up in all the southern countries. We haven't been able to charge him with anything that sticks. But we were not aware that he was back in Zurich. I'll look into it immediately, and I'll get back to you. Give me the number where we can reach you."

Adam could only hear one side of the conversation. He would not leave Friday's side while he was on the phone. Friday was finding it difficult not to show alarm.

"She drowned, didn't she?" Adam kept repeating.

Suddenly Adam pulled a chair beside the table; he laid his head down on his folded arms on the table and began sobbing.

"We don't know that," Friday said, trying to comfort him. Just as he reached over to give him a reassuring squeeze on the arm, Adam got up, ran to his room, slammed the door, and flung himself across the bed. Brutus, who had been lying in the corner studying them, slowly got up, walked in front of Adam's closed door, laid down, and began whining softly.

Weariness enveloped Friday as he tried to concentrate on what he should do next. He went to his room, so tired that his nerves throbbed, and lay on the bed. The next minute he was sound asleep from exhaustion.

The news that no one wanted to hear arrived the next morning when the chief of police called. They had Tony Strumbona in custody. He confessed that he was with Marie on the boat but insisted that she fell overboard.

"She was drunk," Tony repeated.

"We are not closing the case. There are too many things that don't add up, like why didn't he inform anyone? We are talking to everyone who was on the boat that night. We may never be able to recover the body. I'm so sorry for your loss. If anything changes, we will keep you informed," the police chief told Friday.

□□□□□

The month was up. Friday's assignment with Adam was completed. But he couldn't leave now. Adam had no parents, and from what Friday could tell, his grandparents were just too far up in years to provide the care the boy needed. He called Speller, explaining what had happened and how vulnerable Adam was.

Speller understood and advised Friday to stay as long as was necessary.

"Do what you have to do. I'll support you in any way," were his parting words before he hung up.

When Friday called Gram Wilma to tell her what happened, there was a long pause on the phone. He thought he heard a frail voice repeat, "Lordy—Lordy—Lordy."

Friday became alarmed. "Are you still there?" he asked.

"Yes, I heard you," she said.

"Adam and I will be out tomorrow." Friday was not looking forward to the meeting, but it had to be done.

The next morning Adam and Friday were on their way to see Gram and Gramps. They were halfway there when Adam took a deep breath and said, "Friday, I'm afraid!" Tears had welled up in his eyes.

Friday glanced at him. Adam was hunched down in his seat. He seemed small and weak. His clothes looked too big for him. The tears had now overflowed and were shining tracks down his cheeks.

"What are you afraid of?" Friday asked.

"What's going to happen to me? I don't want to be alone." Adam began weeping, shaking from the effects of too much happening, but shaking from something else as well, some dark fear.

"You aren't alone," Friday said.

"I'm afraid that nobody wants me and that I'll be alone."

"You are a great kid; we'll see what Gram and Gramps say, but you won't be alone., Adam."

"I want someone like my dad or mom to be here. It scares me."

"We will find someone."

"I have. You, Friday. I want you to be my big brother or dad, for real. Can you do that?"

Friday was speechless. He kept his eyes on the road, searching for a plausible response.

"You don't want me either," Adam said, his voice genuinely fragile and shaking.

"Whooo, man, you're getting way ahead of yourself. We don't know if your mother really is dead. She's still considered a missing person."

A New Beginning

"She is DEAD," Adam emphasized.

The silence loomed between them like a heavy mist the rest of the way.

Gram Wilma was on the front porch when they drove up. Putting on a brave front for Adam's sake, her mind was a crazy mixture of hope and fear.

"I made your favorite strawberry pie," she greeted Adam.

"Mom's dead. I know it," Adam said. Gram Wilma opened her arms, and Adam ran to her. She held him close and stroked his head as he sobbed. She, too, was close to tears but held herself together.

"You poor child," she moaned. "Gramps is waiting for us inside," she said as she led Adam into the kitchen.

Gramps was at the table staring at his own swollen, gnarled hands on the patterned tablecloth before him. His red-rimmed eyes grew watery, and for a moment, he looked as if he was about to cry. But he blinked rapidly and held back the tears.

In a voice laden with despair, he said, "That poor boy is going through so much grief. God better have a good reason for all of his loss."

Gram Wilma looked at her husband. "James, what a thing to say! We don't know why things happen."

"I figured out the reason," Gramps said.

Friday, surprised by this unpredictable outburst, pulled up a chair by the table and sat down. He wanted to hear what Gramps had to say.

On impulse, Gram Wilma made a quick decision. "Adam and I are going out to the shop. I want to show him something."

James waited until they were gone and began speaking what was on his mind, "This may sound strange, but I've got to have my say. I believe Adam. Marie is dead. I got the same feeling when you first called us. Wilma and I thought this through. We think that you would be the best person to raise Adam. He has no kin. We aren't able to shoulder the responsibility. I have great difficulty caring for myself, and last week the doctor told Wilma she has to start chemo treatments. This is no place to raise a boy who has gone through so much in such a short time. You're young. You can better handle it."

Friday listened, too startled to offer any objection.

"I watched you with the boy when you were out here to fish. Adam looks up to you the same way he did with his father. Fact of the matter is, you remind me of Rob. You have the same kind, concerned and patient way that he had." James studied Friday for a moment and continued. "That's the solution for our Adam—you raising him. The only other thing left is to let the government agency place him in foster care. He deserves better. I said my piece. Now I want to hear from you."

Friday sat bewildered, off guard. So many questions, so much to think about. The room spun with possibilities and scenarios.

"Well, Adam did bring up that solution in the car on the way over here," he said finally.

"So, consider it now. It's a yes or a no. No use waiting around."

"Yes! I want to do it," Friday said without hesitation. His relief and answer gave way to a new mystification. He wasn't so sure the old Alex would have made the same decision before having these new experiences through Speller.

James nodded, smiling. "Now that we got that settled, go get Wilma and Adam. I'm ready for a piece of Wilma's strawberry pie."

They all sat down to enjoy the pie, and Gramps told Adam that Friday wanted to be his big brother and dad for the rest of his life if he would have him.

Adam was overcome with joy, shouting, "Yes! Yes! Yes!"

Before they left for home, Gram Wilma had something to say. She turned to Adam and began with a sad tone in her voice, "You may not realize the significance of what I have to tell you today, but I'm certain you will remember it one day. When something traumatic happens, even time can't always heal it. To understand the purpose, or the 'why' many times, is difficult. One must learn to overcome and accept it as a learning experience.

A New Beginning

After she said her piece, Friday brushed the tears from his face, walked over to her, embraced her, and, looking at Gramps; he said, "The two of you are the most caring people I have ever known. I feel honored to have met you."

On that note, Friday and Adam departed.

◻◻◻◻◻

There were many loose ends that had to be taken care of before the adoption could be finalized.

Frank recommended a responsible attorney.

Kay and Frank were pleased when they heard of Friday's decision to become Adam's dad. Friday and Adam decided that it was best that they give Frank a tape that Adam made. It would help him to better understand and help Oscar.

Gram and Gramps coordinated with Kay to help them with the sale of the house and were most helpful just being there for Adam as they parceled out all of Marie's personal effects.

Friday called Trish on a daily basis, telling her what was happening. She, in turn, reminded him that there are no accidents, no happenstance. "I'm certain," she said, "that Adam was destined to be your son."

The night before they were to leave Round Rock for a new life in Houston, Adam went to bed early, belongings all packed, still keyed up with all the things that had happened in the past two weeks.

Friday went to his room. It was so quiet that Friday could hear his watch ticking on his wrist and his heart beating, and the occasional scrape of a tree branch that brushed against the window pane.

He listened for a noise from Adam's room across the hall.

Nothing.

He sighed, relieved that Adam could finally sleep. It would be a long drive to Houston.

Friday began mentally reviewing all the things that had happened since his arrival in Oklahoma—the one day he would never forget, the day with Gram Wilma and Gramps James, the day that changed his future.

He felt compelled to write Adam a letter.

He began writing:

Dear Adam,

When you read this, you're going to remember everything you told me, and you're probably going to be a little embarrassed.

Don't worry.

What you told me will stay strictly between us. And I'll tell you some outrageously embarrassing secrets of my own, so then we'll be even.

After all, cleaning the soul is one-thing big brothers and Dads are for.

Friday

He slipped the note under Adam's door and went to bed for a good night's sleep. Gram's words came to mind, and he began preparing and vowing to learn and to accept situations even if he did not understand the higher purpose.

☐☐☐☐☐

Adam adjusted to his new surroundings in Houston without any problems.

He not only had a Dad—he had a granddad that doted on him.

After Speller heard Adam play the fiddle, he took him to the private institute in Houston, comparable to Julliard in New York. They accepted Adam for his abilities, encouraging and tutoring him to further his talent. After hearing several of his peers play the violin, Adam decided that this was the kind of music he wanted to play—classical.

Trish came to visit Friday, and their relationship grew. Today, she is Adam's mother. They have a warm, loving relationship. He calls her Mom.

Friday, Adam and Trish go back to Oklahoma often to visit Gram Wilma and Gramps James.

Oscar is in another school, and Frank and Kay are proud of the progress he is making.

A MAN CALLED FRIDAY

Epilogue

ONE YEAR LATER

The man called Friday—Alex Sander—has followed in his father's footsteps. He became a writer and author.

He and Trish built a three-story home with a nest on the third floor. Their home is on fifty acres on the outskirts of Houston.

The nest is Adam's favorite place to practice the violin.

When Olivia and Paul came for Trish and Friday's wedding, Olivia fell in love with Texas. Now retired, she found the perfect acreage not too far from Friday and Trish.

Her plans to build a creative center for talented and promising children is coming full circle. It will be located on her property in Texas. Trish will be her partner.

Paul is still very much in Olivia's life. Who knows, she, too, may have found her soulmate and finally recognized it in Paul.

In Contact With Other Realms

About the Authors

"Let me be a channel to help people help themselves."
Helene Hadsell

HELENE HADSELL

Helene Hadsell's life was proof not only of her dynamic philosophy but also of her practice of positive thinking in the energetic pursuit of her goals, which brought her rich rewards in terms of spiritual, physical, and material well-being. Her books recount the fantastic events of her life and bear out her conviction that anyone can achieve anything their mind can conceive if they firmly resolve to do so.

In 1986, she founded Delta Sciences as a retreat center. People came from all over the world, including England, Switzerland, Hungary, and Peru, as well as from every state in the USA.

Helene Hadsell was the mother of three children: Pamela, Dike, and Chris. She also had three grandchildren and three great-grandchildren. She lived in Alvarado, Texas, with her husband Pat, who shared her interest in helping people improve their lives through mental power.

CAROLYN WILMAN

Carolyn Wilman is a digital marketing specialist who works with companies to create successful sweepstakes marketing campaigns and winning promotions.

Her work as a marketing expert landed her on the cover of Marketing Magazine. She was named by MORE Magazine as one of Canada's Top 40 Women over 40 and was featured in High Stakes Sweepers, a pilot TV series for TLC (previously known as The Learning Channel).

Ms. Wilman is also known as the Contest Queen and author of two best-selling books; *You Can't Win If You Don't Enter* and *How To Win Cash, Cars, Trips & More!*, and has also re-released Helene's other books, *The Name It & Claim It Game*, *In Contact With Other Realms*, and *Confessions of an 83-Year-Old-Sage*.

Carolyn is a single mother of one amazing daughter and resides in Oshawa, Ontario, Canada. Similar to Helene, she believes her purpose in life is to teach others how to have more fun and embrace the grand adventure we call life.